Walkin' the Dog

ALSO BY CHRIS LYNCH

Freewill

Iceman

Gypsy Davey

Shadow Boxer

Killing Time in Crystal City

Little Blue Lies

Pieces

Kill Switch

Angry Young Man

Inexcusable

Walkin' the Dog

by Chris Lynch

Simon & Schuster Books for Young Readers
NEW YORK   LONDON   TORONTO   SYDNEY   NEW DELHI

SIMON & SCHUSTER BOOKS FOR YOUNG READERS
An imprint of Simon & Schuster Children's Publishing Division
1230 Avenue of the Americas, New York, New York 10020
This book is a work of fiction. Any references to historical events, real people, or real places are used fictitiously. Other names, characters, places, and events are products of the author's imagination, and any resemblance to actual events or places or persons, living or dead, is entirely coincidental.
Text © 2024 by Chris Lynch
Jacket illustration © 2024 by Dion MBD
Jacket design by Sarah Creech © 2024 by Simon & Schuster, LLC
All rights reserved, including the right of reproduction in whole or in part in any form.
SIMON & SCHUSTER BOOKS FOR YOUNG READERS
and related marks are trademarks of Simon & Schuster, LLC.
Simon & Schuster: Celebrating 100 Years of Publishing in 2024
For information about special discounts for bulk purchases, please contact Simon & Schuster Special Sales at 1-866-506-1949 or business@simonandschuster.com.
The Simon & Schuster Speakers Bureau can bring authors to your live event. For more information or to book an event, contact the Simon & Schuster Speakers Bureau at 1-866-248-3049 or visit our website at www.simonspeakers.com.
Interior design by Hilary Zarycky
The text for this book was set in Bembo.
Manufactured in the United States of America
0224 BVG
First Edition
2 4 6 8 10 9 7 5 3 1
Library of Congress Cataloging-in-Publication Data
Names: Lynch, Chris, 1962– author.
Title: Walkin' the dog / Chris Lynch.
Other titles: Walking the dog
Description: First edition. | New York : Simon & Schuster Books for Young Readers, 2024.
Identifiers: LCCN 2023005313 | ISBN 9781481459204 (hardcover) | ISBN 9781481459228 (ebook)
Subjects: CYAC: Friendship—Fiction. | Human-animal relationships—Fiction. | Dogs—Fiction. | Dog walking—Fiction. | Family life—Fiction.
Classification: LCC PZ7.L979739 Wak 2024 | DDC [Fic]—dc23
LC record available at https://lccn.loc.gov/2023005313

Walkin' the Dog

1. The Inactivist

IT'S STILL DARK OUT WHEN MY DAD WAKES ME UP.

Things are supposed to go a certain way, and this is *not* that way. He's a commercial fisher, and so should be out of the house for several hours already by the time I wake up. When I get *myself* up, which I'm perfectly capable of doing.

"Louis," he says, leaning way down close and misting me with coffee and bran muffin and fig and orange breath. Fortunately, I love my father and his relatively healthy diet. Later, he smells different. Fisherfolk, yeah?

"I need you, son."

This, along with the darkness, and the absence of my mother from the house, is a bit unsettling.

My dad doesn't need me, or anybody else, really. At least he's never said so before. He's very seafaring that way. It soothes me, his unneediness.

It's technically not true, anyway. He doesn't need me; somebody else does. But Dad needs that somebody else, so there you have it.

"I'm short a man today," he says, "and Old Man Dan is

the only guy around who knows what he's doing and is also available to give me an honest day's work."

Old Man Dan is Mr. Evans. He's one of those guys you hear about who have millions of "fish stories" about the one that got away and the biggest thing that ever swam the sea. Old Man Dan retired from actual fishing without retiring any of the fish stories, or the scent. They say he's got a thing called *trimethylaminuria*. They also say he reeks. Kind of guy my dad avoids in the street or the supermarket aisle on account of those stories more than the smell, so he must be in serious need of Dan's assistance on this occasion if he's prepared to listen to that stuff all day.

"Okay, can I ask why you're telling me this, Dad?" I ask, without really wanting to ask it.

"Because Dan says he can only go out on the boat today if he can get somebody to look after Amos."

Oh no.

Amos. Dan's multi-breed mongrel, who seems less like a real dog and more like a cross between a portly dingo and a badger. Everybody but Dan refers to him as Anus, because of the smell, which reaches you about twenty-four hours before you're anywhere near him.

"Oh, Dad . . ."

"Please, Louis. The poor thing can't be alone for more than a few hours at a time, ever since Dan's wife passed away. You understand, of course. . . ."

Ah, Dad. I mean, I don't think he did it on purpose, but he did it. He can hardly be unaware that his wife, my mother, is in the hospital, as she has been for too many days the past year. He cannot be unaware, but he also cannot have meant to use that as a point of leverage in this conversation.

His fractured face tells me as much. He caught himself off-balance just as badly as he did me.

"I'll do it, Dad," I say, brushing past him both impatiently and affectionately as I climb out of bed. He squeezes my arm, I squeeze his, and we both look away.

When I come out of the shower and make my way sluggishly to the kitchen table, it's still not quite sunrise. My little sister, Faye, is eating a bowl of cereal by the dim, warm glow of the stovetop light. It's a scene I'm not used to, and one I find unexpectedly pleasant. Faye can be a bit harsh under the full glare of day.

I'm thirteen, and Faye is eleven months younger. Irish twins, they call it, but we might as well be the regular kind. She's as old as me in every other way, if not older. There's a family legend that—because Faye was not exactly a planned baby—Dad wanted to name her Daisy. As in, whoops-a-daisy.

"Oh, for cryin' . . . ," Faye exclaims, letting her spoon fall out of her hand and clatter around the tabletop. She's not really that shocked to see me at this hour, but it's still a pretty good show.

I explain the situation to her, how Dad needs a fisher, and that fisher needs a dog sitter.

"*Anus?*" she asks, incredulous, but not really. "Well, I don't know what you showered for, because that's just soap and water down the drain."

"Oh, he's not that bad," I say, because why not just let her swing away.

"Not that *bad*, Louis? Old Man Dan still smells like chum after all these years, and he remains only the second-raunchiest creature in that house. And you're going over there? You know that's what killed Old Lady Dan the Fishwife, don't you? She died of *stench*. It was in the obituary. I read it."

Always good value for money, my sister.

I shrug. It should be noted that I shrug a lot. It's my official state gesture.

"I'm getting paid," I say. "And Dad needs me to help him out. Those are two sound reasons. Throw in kindness to animals and we're well into bonus territory."

Felt like I was doing pretty well, for a homeschooled debater.

"Oh, you're heading into bogus territory, all right," she says. "Seriously bogus. And I love Dad, and animals, as much as you do. But you know what Ma would have to say about that other thing."

I forgot that I wasn't even the best debater in the house.

"She'd say I should do it for free," I moan. "But Ma would have everybody do everything for free, and that's why we're poor."

"Oh, we're not poor, Louis; we're just normal."

"Yeah, well, poor is not gonna be *my* normal, I'll tell you that."

"Fine," Faye says. "Tell me that if you need to tell me that. I need to tell you that Ma is expecting to see you today. So, while you're walking the dog and grubbing the money, you also need to make time for a visit to your mother."

"I can do that."

"Yeah, you can do that."

"Yeah, Faye, that's what I said."

"Right, I was just helping. Sometimes you need help, to, y'know, *do* things."

This is all so wrong. Not *inaccurate*, but wrong.

"Come on, Faye. Not when it comes to Ma."

Ma is a great many great things. Foremost among them is probably *activist*. She's renowned for it. If there's a cause that needs activizing, she's there, and always has been. To the detriment, one might say, of her personal health and well-being. She cares, about everything, more than a rational person should. In my opinion.

By contrast, I have a nickname, and it was first bestowed upon me by that very same activist Ma.

The Inactivist.

Kind of comical, and true enough, if not exactly flattering. I don't much like getting involved.

"Would you have gone to see her today if I hadn't reminded you?"

"Of course I would have. But, anyway, wasn't today supposed to be your day?"

"Ha!" Faye says, pointing through the air between us sharply enough to nearly hurt my chest. Like she bagged me there. Which, possibly, she did.

"What, 'ha'?" I say. "Today was definitely supposed to be your day."

"What, because they're all my day? Because I'm the *girl*?"

My choices here, as I see them, are limited and not good. An honest answer to that does me no favors. Pausing too long while I come up with something better presents its own problems. It's like verbal waterboarding, trying to argue with Faye.

I aim for her not inconsiderable heart as a viable option to battling her intellectually, which is no option at all.

"Faye, I don't like the hospital. It scares me."

She slows down, out of kindness. I'd sort of prefer it if she sped up.

"I know, Louis. And I understand. But, too bad. And anyway, it's not a hospital, so stop calling it that."

She's half-right, which is about 50 percent less right than she usually is. Ma is staying at a place they call the Knoll. But the Knoll is on the grounds of, and functionally a part of, a whole hospital. It's an inpatient program that lasts four weeks. She's done this thing before. Later, if she still needs them, there are outpatient programs that also last four weeks. She won't need them, though. I'm an optimist. Dad says I am *pathologically optimistic*. Meaning, I tend to believe that things are gonna work out, on their own, without any help from me, the way they should. Because they will, that's why.

Ma is in the Knoll as a direct result of the fact that she cares too much. About everything.

That's an insufficient explanation, probably.

She works at a shelter called A Woman's Place. Doesn't just work the place. *Lives* it. One of their managers. Often a night manager, which can be hard going. She's a stellar person, a soldier. The single best person I've ever met, as a matter of fact. All the pain of A Woman's Place—and that is a *world* of pain—is her pain.

She's an inspiration to me. In a way she would never want to be.

Meaning, I'm determined that what happened to her will never happen to me.

The more streamlined story is, she was breaking up a fight at the shelter one night. In the course of things, she slipped and destroyed her knee. Shredded her ACL and MCL. Such is the esteem in which my mother is held in A Woman's Place that everyone on the scene—including the two combatants—dropped everything in order to care for her on the spot.

That care took her eventually to City Medical Center. And to surgery. And to lots of rehab and physical therapy.

And pain. Lots and lots of pain.

And pain*killers*.

Which isn't an altogether accurate word, is it? Pain doesn't die. I have seen pain, and I have never seen it die.

So the pain got to my ma. And the painkillers got to the pain. Then the painkillers got to Ma.

But it wasn't just the knee, was it?

Dad, who has a way with words for a fisherdude, put it this way: Pain got to Ma. But the pain of *pain* got to her more. Everybody's pain got to her.

She cares too much, is what he meant. Like I said.

She broke, is what happened.

The job did it to her. Then being off the job double-did it to her. She couldn't stand being off the job—not helping out. Helping everybody but her.

"Please, Faye?" I say because I'm out of anything more convincing. "Can't you do today?"

"I did yesterday," she says.

"Yeah, but you could do today, right?"

"Right. I could. But I'm not going to."

"Why not?"

"Because I want you to."

"Aw, that's just—"

"And because Ma wants you to."

Rats. And rats and rats again.

"She didn't actually say that. Did she actually say that?"

"She actually said that, Louis. She wants to see you. And for you to see her. She knows you're afraid."

"And she wants to see me anyway."

"Duh, Louis," she says, and with those three syllables wraps up the discussion.

Duh, Louis. She wants to see me *because* I'm afraid. Not *only* because of that, but for sure it's partly because of that.

There's an empty planter affixed to the wall outside Old Man Dan's door. The chipped alabaster face of the planter looks like Helen of Troy or possibly Troy of Troy, since it's just one of those vaguely classical, scuffed-up sculptures. Inside the otherwise empty head are, as promised, one key and one envelope.

WALKIN' THE DOG

The envelope contains cash. My day's pay. I am to feed Amos and then take him for a long walk. He can be left alone for just a few hours, after which I am to return, give him a snack, and walk him again. I can spend as much extra time as I like, playing with him and entertaining him inside the house or out, this morning or this afternoon. As my rate of pay has already been established and deposited into my pocket, that extra-time scenario seems unlikely.

I take the key and insert it into the lock.

It's as if the turning of the key itself unleashes a tornado of soft-boiled garbage from within the house.

It's a very, very stenchy place. Old Man Dan is a nice guy and all, but his home should be condemned. I'm ready to back straight out again when Amos comes practically cartwheeling toward me from the doorway at the far end of the kitchen. Bless his matted soul, in his excitement he can't get any purchase on the linoleum floor covering, and his long nails clatter against it as if coins are raining down from the ceiling.

"Okay, okay, okay," I tell him anxiously, dropping to my knees to hold him down from launching himself at me again and again. "Okay, boy," I say, wrapping my hands around his rib cage and comforting him as much as possible. His heart is thundering like a full field of horses at the Kentucky Derby. He makes a desperation sound that's half bear cub, half goose. He rams his head into me repeatedly like he badly wants me to leave, but pants and slobbers as if he'll kill himself if I do.

There are a great many cute dogs out there. It's probably kindest if nobody tells Amos about them.

He's asymmetrical all over, and his fur is the color and texture of steel wool. He has multiple leakages—and I'll say no more about those. His head looks like he built it himself out of spare parts. His tail makes chewing-gum-snapping noises when he wags it, and he can't seem to not wag it.

He'll smell better one month after he dies than he does right this minute. And now that he's jumped all over me, so will I.

There's a bag of dry dog food on the counter next to the sink and a can of the wet stuff next to that. I gather that I'm supposed to provide the boy a mix of the two, and so I start by tipping some of the noisy nuggets out of the bag and into the stainless-steel bowl. Then I pop open the can of wet.

Oh my. Oh me oh my. This explains a lot. The odor that leaps up to bite me as soon as the can is breached is precisely the same sad something that clings to Amos all over.

He smells exactly like his food. And it's clearly not the higher-shelf, pampered-pooch brand. If he wasn't right in front of me, I'd swear the goop was made of Amos anus.

With some effort I mix the foods together, and it's such a struggle for my senses that I briefly consider not giving it to him. It feels like some sort of war crime to subject him to this muck, but then I turn toward him. He's sitting in classic good-boy style, looking as if his entire skeleton will leap at me out of his mouth if I don't put that bowl down in front of his pulsating snout within the next five seconds.

So I do, and by the time I straighten all the way back up, there is little sign that I, in fact, fed him anything at all. He continues licking away at the bowl as if his favorite flavor is actually cold metal and he just ate the food to get it out of the way. Fair enough, I guess.

I was told that it's imperative to get Amos out-of-doors immediately, right after feeding him. But since my own biological needs must be met in-of-doors, I quickly slip into the bathroom first.

I can't be more than two minutes in there when I get the reality of what *immediately* means in the world of Amos.

When we used to have a garage and Dad would do his own car repairs, there was often spillage of dirty motor oil out there. The cleanup would include mixing sawdust with the manky old thick oil.

So, visually, Amos's gift is very familiar to me. And since it smells exactly the same as everything else about him, so is the odor.

I'm getting accustomed to such things more quickly than I might have anticipated.

There's a river walk not far from the house, and Amos seems comfortable and happy heading that way. Out in the fresher air he becomes quite tolerable. There's a bounce to his uneven steps that indicates a simple good humor about the world around us. He sniffs tree trunks and beer bottles and other dogs all with the same sprightly snuffle before moving on to the next thing. He never tugs too hard on the leash, lingers too long over the odd nasty poop, or attempts to eat anything that may tip the balance of his delicate constitution. He bumbles along with enough happy-to-be-here that I find myself caught up in his positive approach to just walking. And so we walk. And walk, and walk some more.

It's a splashy sunny morning, the air tastes like cream soda, I don't have any pressing schoolwork to get to, and to be fair, both Amos and I could seriously use the exercise.

But none of this is why we're on the conveyor belt to nowhere.

Truth is, I don't want to visit my ma.

I want to want to visit her, but it's hard. I don't have a history of doing things that are hard, and anytime I have done one, it was probably because I had my ma at my back, urging me on. She's great and scary like that.

And now she's the one who needs the urging. She needs to get better. She needs help. She needs, among other things, me. And I'm struggling to even get myself there.

As I'm wrestling with this, and striding more purposefully away from everything—my home, Amos's home, the hospital—the sun gets stronger, the river flows freer, every reason to be out walking becomes clearer. The dog and I both get it.

Until Amos stops in the middle of the footpath. Just stops. I look all around to see what, if anything, has spooked him. There's nothing, as far as I can tell.

"What, boy?" I ask, and I can't believe I'm already one of those doinky people who ask dogs questions.

But, in his way, he answers. He looks up at me for a few concentrated seconds. Then he spins like a pickled four-legged top and heads back the way we came.

"What?" I say. "You wanna go home?"

WALKIN' THE DOG

I'm apparently not done asking him stupid questions, but he is, apparently, done answering them.

We walk briskly and directly, back to Amos's house. And then past it.

"Um, guy," I say, "here we are." It's the first time I have to actually give him a bit of a yank on the chain. It's almost like he didn't want to go home in the first place.

He could be chugging toward my house, which, I don't know how he knows where that is. Or he could be headed beyond. One thing's for sure—wherever he's headed, I'm likewise headed.

Amos is muscular.

After a short period of stupidity, I stop fighting Amos and follow to wherever he thinks I should go.

We've passed his house.

And then my house.

We continue on for the next several blocks toward the place I know now is the *place*.

Ma's place. Amos fairly drags me all the way to where Ma is, where I don't want to be.

He plunks himself down on the sidewalk in front of the Place. The Knoll. Stares up at me.

"No," I snap.

I know he's thinking, *Yes*. I know he is. I also know Ma is staring down at me from her window. I know she is. Between the judgy bookends of the two of them, I'm beginning to feel shame. And by beginning, I don't mean for the first time today. I mean possibly for the first time ever.

I have no qualms about leaving Amos tied to a sapling on the front lawn of the Knoll. Because who's gonna steal him? And also, it gives me a completely reasonable reason for not staying too long.

What? Stop looking at me like that.

Anyway, Amos is perfectly fine with it. He sits serenely by the tree, in excellent view of the window where Ma is staying. She can meet him from afar, which is the distance you want to meet him from.

The woman at the front desk says she's been expecting me, which is quite something, since I wasn't expecting me. She points me the way, to the elevator and to Ma, both of which I know already, but she's way nice and it's time well spent. Suddenly I get the thought that I should spend a bit more of it checking up on Amos. But he's already onto me, and my time-killing delay tactics will not impress him one little bit. Plus, it will mean a twice-walk of shame when he just sends me right back with a steamy stare. I do not wish to become accustomed to shame.

So, I go to the elevator.

It's only four floors. I'm young. I should probably walk. The elevator seems to agree and snaps at my behind just as I pass through the doors. It speeds me against gravity, dangerously fast for a contraption inside a medical facility. Before I know it—no, exactly as soon as I know it—the jerk elevator jerks to a stop and flashes its flash doors open to the fourth floor.

Where Ma stands, right there, as open as those doors to me.

WALKIN' THE DOG

Before anybody can say anything, I charge out and fairly slam into my mother.

I bury myself in her and cry like a soaking sponge all over her. She holds me there. She holds me. Holds me hard. Like I'll never get away. Like a mother holds a kid.

"Why are you crying?" she asks me real quiet-like, to maybe save me a little bit of the embarrassment as she bundles me down the hall toward her room.

"Because I'm not," I sniff sloppily at her.

She laughs.

That's good. She was supposed to laugh. I could almost always get her to laugh before.

Makes me want to weep. With happiness this time, though the difference might not be that obvious. But she'd be able to tell.

When we complete the snuffle shuffle and she closes the door to her room behind us, she starts talking before I'm really ready to talk.

"Lemme show you," I cut her off, and pull her by the hand to the window. "That's Amos," I say, gesturing to the currently very well-behaved dog below.

"You got a dog?" she asks.

"No. It's Old Man Dan's dog."

"You mean Old Man Dan, the only person who smells more like fish than your father does?"

"That's the guy."

"So, what does his dog smell like?"

"He *aspires* to rotting fish."

She leans up close to the window. "Well, he looks rather sweet from here."

"He is sweet. But 'from here' is his best angle."

She goes quiet. She stares out, down at Amos, but farther than that too, as if she can see a few fathoms beneath the ground beneath the dog. She stares for too long. "Maybe we'll get a dog," she says with less enthusiasm than any of the billions of people who have ever said that before.

"That would be great," I say, trying to make up for it with my overenthusiasm.

"So, why do you have him?" Ma asks as she leaves the window to go sit on her bed.

There's a slippery vinyl chair near her, and I take that.

"Because I'm getting paid for it," I say, and regret it before I can even think why.

She pauses. Leans back against the headboard, crosses her legs at the ankles and her hands in her lap. It's gonna be bad.

"Why are you taking money from a poor, lonely old man to take his dog for a walk?"

Ma's like a big version of Faye. If you don't push back right away, she'll have you.

"Because the poor, lonely old man needed me to care for his dog so that he could get paid to do a full day's fishing for Dad."

"Oh, Louis. You know how sly your father can be. He's probably paying Dan in fish heads. You give him back his money right away."

I don't want to upset my mother right at this moment, truly I don't. But this is the very mother who—way more than Dad ever did—taught me to stick up for myself in all situations.

"No," I say.

She crosses her ankles the other way on top of the crisply made bed.

"No, you say?"

"No, I say," I say.

"And is that *all* you say?"

I guess it'd better not be.

"Ma, I'm getting a fair wage, for a fair day's effort. I've heard you say a zillion times that that is all people can ask for in such a world as this. Sounds like you, doesn't it?"

She unfolds her hands and starts patting her thighs gently and rhythmically. It's a thing she does.

"A zillion is an overestimate, don't you think?"

I sit upright in my slippy uncomfortable chair. I mimic her thigh patting.

"Actually, I would call my estimate conservative, Mother."

She giggles, like a kid. That's another thing she does. Ma is a very serious person, but she loves to be teased. To be seen and known and recognized, and to be called out for it. Loves it.

Just as quickly, her face drops, and seriousness returns. She looks away from me, toward the window. It's turning into a frosty white-gray day, and from this angle, looking out the window is looking at nothing.

"When you coming home, Ma?" I ask, probably sooner than either of us is ready for it.

"I'm missed, am I?" she asks dryly.

"Of course you are," I say. "The place is a dump, and the standard of the food is appalling."

I have managed it again, the making her laugh. The house was never spotless when Ma was there. In fact, it's almost certainly cleaner with her not there. She's kind of sloppy, truth be told. And as for the meals . . .

"I eat better here," she says with a weak smile. The laughter, even the smile, requires a lot more effort than usual. A poorly tuned engine that just about turns over, then keeps spluttering out.

"A couple more weeks, is it?" I prompt.

As if I'd asked something else, she quickly responds, "Dogs come here."

"What?"

"Dogs. They let dogs come in sometimes. People have brought them in. I petted a couple of them. Felt good. I enjoyed it. Dogs are wonderful, as it turns out."

"Oh," I say, happy to have something. "Amos. Almost forgot." I walk to the window again, and my heart inflates a couple of sizes at the sight of him. I didn't expect him to take off or anything, but all the same. There he is. I look back toward Ma but point out the window. "Amos," I say vaguely.

"Amos," she repeats vaguely.

"I probably shouldn't leave him," I say.

"Probably shouldn't," she says.

"I can stay a few more minutes," I say, like the wonderful guy I am not.

"Comfort dogs. That's what they call them. And it's true, they're really comfortable."

"I also have schoolwork," I say. "As you know. Faye is a taskmaster. Does she really need to be in charge, Ma?"

"She's not actually in charge, Louis," she says with a tut. "But yes, she really does."

Her phone rings. Because, you'll see.

"Hiya, sweetheart," Ma says to the rotten little gadget. That is not a reference to the phone, incidentally.

"Yes," she says, "he's here."

"No, I'm not," I hiss urgently. "I mean, I was here, like she told me to be, but I'm not now. Tell her that. Tell her both of those things."

Why should I be this scared of someone who does not weigh ninety pounds?

"He's not here, Faye." She sounds like she's reading an eye chart. "He was here, like you told him to be. But he's not now."

I make the slog from the window back to the bedside chair and hold out my hand. "Thank you, secretary," I say. "I'll take this call."

"Good," Ma says. "I like it better when you get along."

"Why didn't you just call me directly, Faye?" I ask.

"What, you would have answered?" she quanswers. That's a word she herself made up, for answering a question with a question.

"I don't have to quanswer that," I say.

"Okay, right, fine," she says. "I really just wanted to be sure you made it by there, but honestly, you do need to get home and do some coursework."

"Right," I say. "Fine," I say.

I don't like this, at all, that I'm taking directions from my little sister, and not my mother, and especially ... not my mother.

"Ma," I blurt, dropping her phone on the bed next to her, "why can't you come home? Like, now? Like, *right* now? I can take you home. I can walk you right home, me and Amos together, and you'll be safe, and comfortable, and whatever. You seem fine and healthy, Ma. You *look* great, and fine and healthy, and I don't understand why—"

Faye, or anyway the flat little electronic version of her, is howling from her spot there on the bed, and I'm pretty sure I can hear my name coming up out of her in that small, powerless voice and something like, "... and you stop that right this minute or I swear I'm gonna ..."

And she will, too. Whatever she's threatening to gonna do to me, she will, and successfully.

I should talk to her.

"You should talk to her," Ma says.

I talk to her.

"Louis," she hisses insistently, "you have to leave her alone. She's there for a reason, because she needs to be there and because they're making her better. The fact that you don't understand—as you don't understand many things—is not really important here."

With my obviously limited powers of understanding, I shouldn't really be able to get what she's saying. But I do get it. I know, inside, that Ma needs to be where she is for now. I also know that I'm struggling with it and that I feel helpless, powerless, everything-less when Ma is away.

I wish I could do something. Even though I famously don't much like doing things.

"You're right, Faye," I say.

"I am?" she says.

That felt pretty good, catching her off guard like that.

"Yeah. In fact, I'm coming home right now. Looking forward to seeing you, too."

"Oh, right," she says, "now you're just being—"

She's right, I am. I hang up on her to underscore that point.

Faye greets me, nose-to-nose, at the kitchen door when I get there. As if she knew I brought company.

"I smelled him blocks away," she says. "*Anus* is not coming in here, Louis."

"Well," I say, "he is. He has to. Don't you care about our mother?"

"What? Yeah. What?"

"It's for comfort. For Ma. Turns out they allow comfort dogs there at the Knoll. And Ma would like one. And Amos isn't getting through the front door without a thorough bathing. And that, dear sister, is a two-person job. As I'm sure you'll agree."

Faye is so uncharacteristically quiet. It's delicious, watching the whole hands-on-hips, sighing-at-the-ceiling, waving-us-in-like-a-traffic-cop surrender.

"Boy, do we love our mother," Faye says, with her hands cupped defensively over her nose and mouth.

"Boy, do we," I say.

2. Adaptability

THERE'S A REASON IT'S NOT AN ENTIRELY BAD THING WHEN Dad's in charge. The why of it is absolutely a bad thing. Ma being unwell. But looking for a bright side is something I can do, and I'm pretty accomplished at that. Adaptability, I think, is about the most useful trait a person can have in this *thing* of a world, and so if you really pay attention, the *thing* itself will teach you how to get along and get by.

Unlike Ma, Dad is not anti-money. Material wealth is neither his enemy nor his bedfellow. He has just never been very good at acquiring it or hanging on to it once he did. He doesn't care enough about it, is the thing. As I understand it, that's considered a fine character trait. I'm kind of on the fence about that.

Dad's actual bedfellow would not agree with either of us.

Ma cares about money, a lot. The same way cats care about rats and vice versa.

"Money stinks!" is my mother's most famous and frequent proclamation on the subject of American capitalism.

It was by design that we never had any money. Maybe not

by design, exactly, but surely by our undeclared war on wealth.

So, we once lived in a city, a real, serious, all-in, all-out city, full of every variety of people and things and experiences that give a person a genuine crack at having stuff happen to him. Because if you live in a place like that, things will eventually happen to you. They just will.

Then we moved here. It's nearer to the ocean but farther from absolutely all else. A place where every last person has a limp, like a pirate retirement community. And one out of every three plays the harmonica. Most of them unpleasantly.

We left because of my brother, and my father. They reached a point where they no longer got along with the city, if they ever actually had. So Ike's gone from rotten city punk to aspiring townie cop, and Dad's gone fishin', literally. He was a firefighter before coming here to fish commercially.

Dad was in the fire service for twenty years, before he tired of it. Or, as he put it, the service tired of him. He took early retirement, because the whole fireman gig had changed beyond all recognition from when he joined up.

Some people said it needed to change. Dad was not one of those people. The story of our relocation is in a way the story of my father's relationship with the world. In the city, it got too big, too gnarly, too anxious, too *much*. Dad came here in search of more quiet, and less of everything else.

Ike, now, Ike is a police cadet, an officer of the law. He likes to call himself a peace officer, because he is also a laugh-and-a-half. He's training as a motorcycle cop. He's also a motorcycle civilian.

Ike likes bikes.

But nobody likes Ike.

That's not true. I like Ike, more than I don't. Having him for a brother is like having one of those scary, dangerous dogs who might very well turn out to be a face-eater. But there is comfort in knowing that he's probably not gonna eat *your* face. And he has a smattering of other friends, now anyway, mostly law enforcement or motorcycle types, or both. Noisemaker people. Probably for the best, because you can always hear them coming. And you always want to hear guys like them coming.

Back in high school, nobody liked Ike.

That's not really true either. For sure there was plenty of no-like-Ike to go around, and that was proven by his many scars and suspensions, which he acquired largely through fighting people. But even he would admit that he wasn't going around fighting *everybody*. By his own reckoning, Ike fought guys who were not a lot like Ike. Didn't look like him, didn't sound like him, didn't act like him, didn't think like him.

In Ike's opinion, he was guilty of the crime of being Ike, and nothing else.

Curious, wouldn't you say?

Curious is what Ike would say, and does say frequently. That's funny for two main reasons. One is that Ike does curious things on practically an hourly basis. The other is the way he says the word *curious*. He pronounces it like there's no letter *r* in the middle. *Cue-eous*. Because of the wormy, thick scars running diagonally across the front of his lips and the nerve damage that came along with them. That's what a steady diet of mouth-knuckles will do for ya.

Were the scars *them*, because of the two chops across two lips, or were they a *the*, because it was clearly one good gash interrupted by one mouthy mouth?

Doesn't matter, probably. Especially since Ike doesn't acknowledge the situation at all. Unless he's faking it, he doesn't even know he has the minor impediment to his speech.

Curious.

I never bring it up, and never intend to.

Because here's the thing, or *a* thing anyway, an important thing: no matter what other people think my brother may be, and no matter what my brother may, in fact, be, he has always been something different to me. Something more complex. At least some of the time.

Doesn't make other opinions wrong, though. I know that.

Could all these things be right at the same time? Possibly. Probably.

They are not the same, however. Somehow, they are very, very, very different. Numerous somehows.

Like how Ike went to the public high school in town, and I didn't. Like how when he was growing up, we still lived in that town, which is actually a midsize city but is and always will be a town. The Town. Like how when he graduated, just about, from that school, it was as if the entire family graduated from the Town. Within one month of the grand occasion when the family failed to witness Ike receiving his diploma. Because none of us went to the ceremony. Because my brother himself couldn't be bothered. We packed up the wagon train and moved ourselves forty miles, and several styles, away, out of the Town and onto the coast.

Gotta think that's a pretty bad experience, a school life so sour that your entire family relocates at the end of it just not to be reminded. My folks have always maintained that that's not what it was about. But it's hard not to notice that the way life has been for Faye and me compared to what Ike experienced could hardly be incidental or accidental.

For his part, Ike barely seemed to notice. He moved out again a month after we moved in. He says now that he never even lived here.

He did. For a month. You cannot rewrite parts of life. Not even little parts. They all matter, and they all contribute to the whole of things.

Like spatchcock chicken.

Spatchcock chicken has always been an integral part of life in this house. The savage carnivorous part of the family—that would be everybody but Ma—eats a fair amount of chicken generally, but the entrée that is spatchcock holds a special place for us, bless its butterflied soul.

The sound of it alone has generated more laughter around here than it has any right to.

Dad pretty much never doesn't laugh when he says it.

Ma would never eat it, but I think she might slaughter the bird herself, just for the daffiness it produces in my father.

Which is why we're having a batch of the spatch for supper tonight. It's Tuesday, and our Tuesday ritual is that we all have dinner together. Even Officer Ike, who, remember, doesn't live here and never did. Even if he did.

We also have a special guest star, brought to us live from the Knoll via video call and tablet. Propped up on a mini easel at one end of the dining room table.

"Hey, Ma," Ike calls out, waving the quickest and most enthusiastically when she appears on-screen. Because he's the one who visits her the least. Everyone wishes he would visit her more. Everyone has told him so.

Ike does not like to be told. Anything.

"Hello, everyone," Ma says, warmly but weakly. She sounds like she's just climbed a long flight of stairs to reach us.

"Spatchcock chicken," Dad blurts with unsettling enthusiasm. He holds the roasting pan up close to the tablet, so that maybe she can smell it.

"Ah," she says, pointing at it and waving.

Not right, is it? Nothing's right.

Naturally it's down to Faye, up to Faye, to try to pull things together.

"Have you eaten, Ma?" she asks, sounding like she knows the answer already and is not happy with it. "You have to eat, even if the food's not great. You look pale. You sound tired."

"I was just thinking that same thing." She frowns hard, reaches out to poke the screen. "This thing. It's not very good, is it? Makes me look bad, and sound bad. That's not really me."

It is, though.

"How do I look on your end?" Dad asks her. "Old? I bet it makes me look old."

This is a gag that's been running longer between them than spatchcock chicken. Dad *is* old. He's got a dozen years on Ma, and they've had plenty of fun with that over the years. Everyone has. Being a tree hugger, Ma often said she only married him because once he cut his hand badly and she was able to count his rings and she was wildly impressed yet sympathetic.

"Old," she says. "It's just the unforgiving technology, but yes, it's making you look old."

Dad makes himself busy passing food around to everybody, and we try as much as possible to act like this is a family meal. Contrary to what it's supposed to achieve, the video dinner seems to be taking a lot out of both of them. He leans into it, though.

"It's not the technology, sweetheart, unless it's the fact that it's too good, too clear and accurate. Did you forget how old I am? My first pet when I was a kid was a velociraptor."

We've all heard that one many times. When Ma laughs as if she hasn't, we're all thrilled to be hearing it again.

The gaps in conversation quickly grow. It's easy and uncomfortable to tune in to the sounds of cutlery when dinner-table chatter fails to keep up. It sounds gross to me, strangely savage, like we're animals. Though animals using silverware would be doing a commendable job of *not* being savage, actually.

"Thank you for bringing Amos," Ma chirps suddenly. "Everybody here has been raving about him since his visit. Such a sweet creature he is."

"Oh," I say, "that's so great to hear. I think he had a fine time too. Y'know, I could bring him by again tomorrow. That would be no—"

"No," she says more firmly than she has said anything else.

"Why not?"

"Because I have something more important I want you to do."

Without even knowing what it is, I go into my default mode. "Why can't Faye do it?"

"Because Faye would be happy to do it."

I'm already frustrated. "That makes no sense," I say.

"I'm guessing it's something that will produce some common good," Faye says, giving me a wink Ma can't see.

"Aw," I moan. "Is it? Ah, it is, isn't it?"

Ike laughs raucously, showing, very much on purpose, a mouthful of peas and carrots.

"It will do you, and the world, good," Ma says.

I lean into my argument, physically, and am about to protest, when Dad smacks his knife and fork down firmly on the table. Not a demonstrative man, my father. This, and the glare, ends the debate.

My mother's idea is an idea I do not think much of from the start.

WALKIN' THE DOG

The next morning, I should be settling in post-breakfast for a spell of reading and writing, like I usually do. Unlike Ike, Faye and I have been homeschooled for the past several years, and to be honest, it's suited me fine all the way. I like to be home. If you have a decent home, why wouldn't you want to be there? I think it would be weird if I didn't feel that way. It's summer now, but with this arrangement, even summer school isn't bad.

Especially since it's all coming to an end, at least for me. When the new school year starts, I'll be out of the house and into the high school . . . not my choice, by the way. So I'm savoring every last day of this life.

It's been a lot of things, technically, blended together into our own thing. We've been non-schooled, virtual schooled, paired-up schooled with actual schools. But mostly, it's been homeschooling for us, and the schooler herself has been Ma. She's done a fine job of it, and all you need for proof is the fact that I really like to be homeschooled. I really like to be *home*. And now, with my new, unexpected sideline in professional dog care, my days are shaping up to be full and fulfilling and profitable. Just walk a dog correctly once or twice and see how quickly you become in demand.

I like being in demand. As long as it's not too demanding.

Which is why I'm protesting. From the breakfast table. I'm protesting being sent out to protest.

"I'm not a protester, Ma," I say as I field my literal marching orders. I miss my mother terribly, but I think if this hologram version starts materializing at every meal, it could get difficult. "I don't even get it, mostly. The protesting business. Does anything ever come of it? Does anything ever happen? What's the point? The world, the country, the universe, have all been doing just fine without my two cents so far, and there's no reason they won't continue doing fine without it."

"Doing *fine,* Louie?" she yodels at me as I try to peacefully polish off my bagel. She says my name without the *s* at the end, as if we're French. We are not French. I'd prefer the *s* were pronounced. "Doing *fine?* You look around at this moment in history and you see *fine?* Dear god, where have I been failing you all these years?"

"You have not been failing me," I say, now getting a bit agitated—on her behalf. "You've done a great job, Ma. I'm plenty smart, and more importantly, I know how to keep getting smarter. I know how to learn, and wasn't that the point all along?"

"Yes, but it means nothing if you are too . . . timid . . . or apathetic . . . or spoiled to get out there and invest yourself in what's going on."

We don't do this. We never do this. Not like this. It has me jangling with nerves to the point where my hands are visibly pulsating.

"What's the big deal, Ma?" I ask, trying to lower the volume and the temperature.

"The big deal, son, is lessons. There are the lessons you take here at home, and they are important. But there are other lessons, important lessons, waiting for you out there in the wider society. I am sending you out so that you can experience bigger things. I want you to be a presence at those bigger things."

Bigger things on this day involves people being seen and, more so, being heard.

My mother would normally be the one to go to something like this, because that is exactly the type of mother, the type of citizen, that she is. She has, like, a swollen empathy gland or something that causes her to feel every bit of every pain or injustice that comes rambling by, whether it's addressed to her or not. This one, though, she has to miss for very obvious and substantial reasons. Faye would go, but that's not what Ma wants.

A decent son would be doing this without a word of back talk.

But since all she's got is me—Ike doesn't count—I have to go, to represent her.

It's rare that I manage to exasperate my mother, but it's not impossible. "Stop pouting, and quit with the drama," Ma finally says. "You don't even have to *do* anything."

I just about manage to stifle a big fat honest "Well, at least there's that."

Ma continues. "I'm not sending you to protest. I'm just sending you to *witness*, son. Be a witness to your world. The world needs witnesses. The bad guys do their baddest when there are no witnesses."

3. Biomed Beagles

THE EVENT IS MA ALL OVER. IMMIGRATION IS PILING A bunch of families onto a plane bound for Guatemala, which doesn't sound like such a bad thing to me, but they don't want to go. If I could take somebody's place on that plane, I seriously would. Not because I'm some kind of do-gooder hero, since I'm no such thing, but because I think I would like to visit Guatemala.

But first I need to visit Anus. It's a regular gig now.

Old Man Dan has quickly gotten used to my presence in his aromatic life. I make Amos happy, and that makes Dan happy. Dan pays me, and that makes me happy. It's an example of what my mother taught me is called a virtuous circle. Okay, I may have modified her definition of virtuous a little, but close enough.

After a quick spin around town with Amos, I'm bringing him home and trying, *trying* to psych myself up for witnessing the demonstration. Dan, bless him, opens the door before we get there and welcomes Amos with dangerous affection. The two of them wind up rolling around on the kitchen floor, as if I were some kind of dognapper rather than a reasonably well-compensated small businessdude.

Not sure about the chemistry of it all, but somehow the mingling of the two old dogs produces an aroma that is way beyond the sum of their farts. We'll call the scent smellderly. I almost find myself backing away from the money when Dan pops up from the floor and walks toward me with some crisp green.

"Thank you, Mr. Evans," I say.

"Don't thank me; thank him," he says, gesturing over his shoulder toward the dog with his whole face in the water bowl. He's not even drinking.

"Well, thank *you*, Mr. Evans," I say.

Amos raises his head in my direction, dripping water all over the floor.

"Oh, you made his day," Old Man Dan says. "He loves to be called that."

I shake my head, grinning at the two of them because you gotta, dontcha? "I'll be off then, guys," I say.

"Hold on," Dan says. "Do you still have spaces on your client list?"

Client list? Sweet, I'm already way more important than I was when I left the house.

"I could possibly squeeze somebody in," I say, "assuming you're recommending them."

"Well, I am," Dan says. "More importantly, Amos has been talking. To his friends."

I'm fairly sure Dan believes it when he says stuff like this.

"Only good things, I hope," I say, wagging my finger, like a doof.

"Of course," he says convincingly, "only the good. We keep the other stuff to ourselves."

Okay, you're losing me now there, Dan.

"Who's this client, then?" I ask.

"Hold your horses," he says. "I think when we bring you new business, we should get a reduction in our rate." The *we* thing is pretty cute. But I see how it could become less cute rapidly.

"You mean, there may be more clients out there you could hook me up with?"

"Could be," he says, "could be. First, the financial arrangement."

Wow. No flies on Old Man Dan. Well, no metaphorical flies, anyway.

"Let's start with this first referral," I say. "Then we can talk about revising the arrangement afterward. So, where do I need to go?"

"You'll be pleased. It's a very short trek."

"Excellent, that's my favorite kind of trek."

Dan smiles and points me toward the house directly across the street. "Tell 'em Amos sent you," he says.

"Yessir, I will," I say, hop-skipping across the street. I'm just about to press the doorbell when I remember—if I ever honestly forgot—that right now I'm supposed to be on my way to a very different, nonpaying gig.

It's okay. It'll be okay. If it's an important demonstration, it'll be on the news, and I can *witness* it there. And if it's not important enough for their time, why is it important enough for mine?

I'll watch it later. I'll take notes. CliffsNotes protesting, that's for me. Lessons will be learned.

Ding-dong.

The door opens and I'm greeted by a smiling woman who looks like both George and Martha Washington.

"Oh," she says brightly, "you'll be Louis, then."

"I will be," I say, managing not to add that I will be whoever you want as long as you hire me.

"We've heard wonderful things about you," she says.

"Really?" I say before needing to reel back any unfortunate honesty. "Oh, right, dogs. You can get them to say anything for a little piece of a sausage."

"Oh, you're a scamp," she says, leading me inside.

"I'm a scamp," I say, following her inside.

Like a dog, I suppose I'll say anything for a price too.

There's an older gent sitting on a sofa in the living room when we walk in. He's like a far more sanitary version of Old Man Dan, and there is one beagle up on the sofa with him and another on the floor, staring straight up as if he wishes he could be there too. The place is flowery. Everything is covered in fat-bloom flowers, either real or human-made. The couch, chairs, rug, wallpaper. The dining room table behind the man. The tablecloth lying between the table and the vase. Every windowsill flowers with blossoms. The place even smells more like flowers than dogs, and that's a pleasant change from my regular. No offense, dog pals and dog people.

"Willard," the woman says, "this is Louis."

Willard flails around a bit to try to get up to greet me. The dogs do nothing to make it easier for him.

"Please, don't get up, sir," I say, scooting up and shaking his hand right where he is.

He shakes my hand, firmly and seriously. Judging from the might of his grip and several old photographs arrayed on the upright piano on either side of the other vase, I'm guessing this is a military man.

"Y'like dogs, do ya?" Willard says to me as I squat down to pat the beagles.

"Woof," I say.

"Good," he says. "Good, that's good." He doesn't smile. Not with his face, not with his voice, not with his manner. The floweriness of the house does not come from Willard. "Get the boy a cookie, Virginia, will ya?"

"I was just about to," she says, smiling for both of them. I bet that skill comes in handy. "I was waiting for the introductions to be over."

"Louis," he says, stroking the dog on his hip, "this is Magnolia, but you can call her Maggie. And this rascal here on the floor is Buckminster, but you can call him Bucky. There, introductions."

The word *rascal* gets an uncommon workout here, I gather. Virginia hops happily toward the kitchen, pushing her way through one of those old-fashioned swinging doors. With everything, I'm half expecting a cowboy to get slung through that door any second.

"Ever heard of biomed beagles, Louis?" Willard says.

"No, sir," I say.

"They're bred, from birth. From pre-birth, even, to be used in medical experiments. Temperament's a big part of it. They're cursed for being sweethearts, essentially."

"Story of my life," I sigh.

Do I want to hear this, though? I don't want to hear this. Maybe I need to hear this? Jeez, Virginia, how long does it take to rustle up a cookie? *Rustle up?* Where'd the cowboy stuff come from all of a sudden? Y'know, once I get a simple thought, it's simple thoughts all the way....

Focus, Louis, focus. It won't be that bad.

"Sometimes a medical trial or a study goes down," Willard says while his wife holds my cookie hostage in the kitchen. "Then the dogs become orphaned, waiting to get rescued by the likes of us. Whatever their state or what stage of the study they happen to be at."

She's not coming. Virginia is not coming back until this story gets good and told. She's heard it before and doesn't care to hear it one more time. And she doesn't want to watch while somebody like me hears it all new again.

I hurry things along.

"So, sir, you'd like me to walk them for you, is that right? I can do that, no problem."

With some effort, and some resistance from Magnolia, he stands. She gets up as well but stays defiantly on the couch for a bit.

Buckminster tries to get up and join along as Willard

walks deliberately toward the front window for a quick hit of neighbor-peeping. Bucky can manage, just about. He drags himself along the flowery carpet, his front legs doing all the heavy lifting while his back ones try. They scrabble but don't get him up. It's as if they've been told that they can move around but aren't allowed to accomplish anything.

The one dog poses up on the couch, while the other surrenders flat to the floor.

"See, Maggie was in for cardiovascular medication studies," Willard says as he returns to the couch, "while Bucky was in for prosthetics."

That's the sentence that does it.

Virginia, rather than some dusty cowboy, comes blopping through the swinging door. "Who's for cookies, then?" she says like a not-so-sad song.

Willard, Maggie, Bucky, and I all respond in the affirmative to cookies.

"I made them myself," Virginia says unnecessarily. She passes them around, and they're amazing. Not the way great cookies are typically amazing. Amazing, like *what is this?* amazing. Majestic, velvety, textured oatmeal dollops that melt in your mouth and also scratch deliciously at your tongue and tonsils simultaneously. And she has managed to straddle the species, embedding people-friendly raisins in there right alongside some kind of savory chips that I think must be . . . jerky? The perfect human-dog hybrid treat.

The small tea party is a wonder. We love our various

cookies, but I start getting edgy. I want to do my job, and let them know so.

"Will I walk the dogs, then?" I ask.

"Ah, yes, but no," Willard says. "It's about Maggie. She still needs a lot of exercise, but Bucky, poor boy, is not quite up to it. Neither are we, frankly." He makes a sweeping gesture over himself, his wife, and his floor-bound beagle.

"Oh," I say. "Sure. Okay. I'm more than happy to take Maggie out while the rest of you relax. That's kind of what I'm for."

"Oh, well," Willard says, "you can take Virginia for a walk anytime you like. Leave the dogs behind, even, if you want to."

The most shocking part, to me, is the airy way he says it. Unless it's the way she responds.

"And I'd go with him too," she says. "Might never come back, neither, ya crusty old grunt. Serve ya right, it would."

I'm harnessing up Maggie for our walk when Willard starts beckoning Virginia over to him. First smile I've seen on him yet.

"And it would, too, serve me right," he says as he pulls her down to him on the couch. "Cry me eyes out, I would."

As Maggie and I head out, Virginia tells me, "Magnolia sure *loves* her walkin'. You can take Bucky sometime. He has the cutest little wagon wheels for his backside...."

Oh no. *Wagon wheels, beagle backside* . . . C'mon, Maggie, let's giddyup outta here before I say something rassin' frassin' ridiculous.

. . .

Maggie and I don't get more than six minutes out of the house before she drops to something slower than a crawl. She's breathing heavily. Not like panting, but like, complaining, resisting. It's a very scratchy sound, from deep within her bio-beagle lungs.

It's a busy road. There are loads of great dog walks in this town, and I know them all by now. This is not one of them. This was supposed to be a road on the *way* to one of the better roads.

"Whatsa matter, hon?" I ask from my one-knee perch, with our twitchy noses pressed nearly together. If she's trying to tell me anything, it's surely, Magnolia does not *loves her walkin'*.

Since she's not forthcoming with words, it's left to me to conclude that what the matter is, is this walk was not ever her idea. Being a dog walker to a dog that doesn't want to be walked might be a strain on my skill set.

More questions for Maggie occur to me. "You wanna stop? You wanna go home? You wanna go someplace else?"

All she seems to wanna do is plunk down right where we are. Here on the unlovely, toxic road we're on, on a rise overlooking ice cream trucks and minivans and motorcycles that are too loud.

"You wanna just sit here?" I ask, after the question's already been answered. We plunk our two bony bottoms on the patchy grassy verge and watch the traffic grumble by. She seems content to do that, her head even gently swaying back and forth with the motion of the vehicles until I join her in it. Soothing. After maybe ten minutes, her attention drifts elsewhere, to the ground a few feet ahead and to the left of us. If this were another dog, I might get nervous about her potentially somersaulting down into harm's way. But she's not another dog, and so somersaulting is not on the agenda.

What is, however, is a little creature. This road is well known as one of those *splat* alleys, where small mammals, turtles, salamanders, and the like get famously flattened on their way to the river, which runs parallel a few hundred yards yonder. There was a movement some time back, to force the local authorities to make the road more critter-friendly by digging a series of tiny underpasses to get everybody safely across. Local paper called it Toad-al Mayhem. It was funny for about six seconds. They ran with it for six weeks.

Maggie is expressing fascination, in the kind of low-energy way a dog like her would do. She barely bothers to rise up off her belly as she scooches like a sniper along the ground. Once she reaches her destination, she settles in. Staring, sniffing, nuzzling at the thing.

I do basically likewise. Then I'm right up beside her, shoulder to shoulder—are those shoulders, what dogs have?—as we consider our new little friend.

He's plump, greenish, brownish, almost exactly the size of the palm of my hand. He's rough, and dry, so not a frog, then. He's a very serious-looking gentleman. I'm only guessing, of course, but he's giving off some male attitude. Also, what does it matter?

Within seconds I get as drawn in as Maggie. Our noses are both close to touching distance from the toad and each other. For his part, the toad is unimpressed and undisturbed. Until Maggie goes to the next level. She nudges him with her nose, and I simultaneously pull back.

Looks like there could be a confrontation. I'm not too proud to admit I find that a little bit exciting. I suppose the toad's not the only one giving off a male vibe.

"Better watch out," a voice says from so close behind me that it sends me half-barrel-rolling down the embankment toward the traffic below.

I don't want her to know what a fright she gave me, though she may have worked that out anyway from my undignified tumble. "Watch out for what?" I say, casually getting to my feet and slickly refusing to brush off the bits of turf clinging to me.

"For that," she says, pointing to Maggie's intensity. "It's a dog-eat-frog world out there, y'know."

She's gymnast small, this girl. But her face is my age, maybe a year older. She has camel hair hair, and it's wrapped into this big, thick braid that falls forward over her left shoulder. I like braids.

"Well," I say, sounding not exactly like a know-it-all, but maybe a know-pretty-much-most-of-it. "It's actually a toad, but not everybody would know that."

"Huh," she says, squinting like for a better look. "I coulda sworn it was a dog."

I probably shouldn't admit that I almost gave her a straight-up reply to that. Whew.

"Ah," I say instead, "I see what you did there. Good one."

"Actually, though," she says, "a toad is technically a type of frog. But not everybody would know that."

It occurs to me that a battle of wits with her might not be in my best interests. The way she wears this one-side uptick of a smile, like her face is sponsored by Nike, suggests she already knows this.

"You kinda remind me of my sister," I say.

"Why?" she says. "Is your sister awesome?"

I decide to bow out gracefully and with honor. I walk up to where Maggie is actually opening her mouth, jaws just parted over the toad. I give the girl her due.

"You're pretty sharp," I say, "almost like a guy."

"You're pretty sharp too," she replies, "not at all like a guy."

I figure that's as honorable and graceful as it's gonna get, so I start leading Maggie back up the embankment.

"See ya," I say.

"See ya where?" she says, though she could answer that herself, since she's walking right along with Maggie and me.

"See ya here?" I suggest, gesturing at the ground we're walking on. "And there?" at the road ahead toward Maggie's place.

"Okay," she says brightly. I guess it was a conversation. She's like some kind of wood sprite, sprung up out of nowhere and now a part of our little crew.

"I'm Agatha," she says as we walk.

"I'm Louis," I say. "Pleased to meet you."

"What's your dog's name?"

"Her name's Magnolia."

"That's lovely."

"It is. She's not my dog, though."

"Why do you have her, then? Did you steal her?"

"I did not steal her. I am a professional dog walker, I'll have you know."

"Get outta town. And here I was thinking you're just a kid."

"I'm that, too," I say.

"Renaissance dude," she says. "Very impressive."

I guess it's true that I need to get out more often. Meeting people is surprisingly fun.

"Stick around; there's plenty more where that came from," I say as we walk up the path to Magnolia's house.

"Maybe I will," she says just before the door opens.

I know it was my invitation, but did she have to accept it so eagerly?

Virginia must have seen us through the window. She looks delighted to see the three of us.

"It's them, Willard," she calls over her shoulder. "And he's brought his girlfriend."

"Oh," I say, "no—"

"Is she nice?" Willard calls.

"She looks nice," Virginia says. "Looks like that Greta Thunberg from the TV."

"The one that was in *Casablanca*?"

"No, that was Ingrid Bergman."

"She looks like Ingrid Bergman? He's doing very well for himself, then. Not that good-lookin' a boy, y'know."

"*Willard!*" she shouts. "Don't be rude. He can hear you."

"Ah, he knows what he looks like. Pay the boy and get our dog back now."

Why do people make it sound like a hostage situation? For her part, Maggie has plunked her rump on the step between Agatha and me, as if she doesn't recognize this as her destination.

"Willard's late for his nap," Virginia says by way of soothing my feelings.

As Virginia digs around in her purse, Bucky comes cruising past behind her, his famous back wheels moving him at a good clip. He doesn't even pause to greet us as he whirls on, his front paws pounding the carpet like he's punching a speed bag.

Agatha lets out a yelp of delight. "Cutest thing I ever saw," she says.

"His name is Buckminster," I say.

"Oh my *god*," she says.

Virginia pays me, Magnolia sighs and toddles into the house. We make arrangements for further walks this week, and we're on our way again.

"It was a bit soon," Agatha says, "but I was happy to meet your parents."

"Those were *not* my parents," I say.

"Well, they were nice anyway. What should we do now?"

"We? Um . . ."

Sounds like a simple enough question, doesn't it?

Except, I don't think I've ever heard it before. Not precisely.

What should we do now? I mean, who would have ever asked me that? I may never have been part of a *we* before. Not for a long time, anyway. There's Faye. There's Ike. But I can't even imagine them asking me that question. We don't ask. We just do whatever we do.

There were other kids, I suppose. In the early years, when I went to preschool and early primary school, out in the world with other people. I had friends then. Don't exactly remember, though I must have.

Maybe there are some things about homeschooling that have left holes in my experience. Maybe.

"Um . . . ?" Agatha asks.

Lacking much in the way of history to fall back on here, I fall back on simply what I *like*.

"Pizza?" I say.

She perks way up. Beams, in fact. It's almost overwhelming, since it was just my safety-net answer.

"You're lucky that we live in a country where pizza is a verb," she says. "And that it's an answer to the question, what should we do now? And that I really, really, really like pizza."

I pause, a long time, and not on purpose.

"I do feel lucky," I say.

"I can hardly remember the last time somebody offered to buy me pizza," she says.

Pause. Long time. Not on purpose.

"Did I offer to do that?" I ask.

WALKIN' THE DOG

"Well, of course you did, silly. First, you're obviously a gentleman. Second, you just got handed a pile of cash. I was right there. I saw it. And you already owe me for the work I did for you."

"Wh-wh-wh-what?? What work did you do?"

"Same as you. I walked along in the general vicinity of a dog, saw her home safely, and pleased her owners just by interacting with them. Fair play to you, getting folks to give you money for that."

Pause. Long time. Longer time. Entirely on purpose.

This shouldn't be so hard. Why is this so hard? She seems like a good kid, good company, why not hang around with her for a while?

"I'm supposed to meet my sister," I say, having no idea at all where that one came from.

Apparently, this doesn't sound as bizarre to Agatha as it does to me.

"Great," she says. "So meet her. Meet her at the pizza place. Then I can meet her too. You said she's awesome, right?"

I didn't say exactly that, but anyway. The suggestion isn't a bad one. I already feel a little less anxious about going out for early pizza with this person I hardly know. This girl person I hardly know.

I take out my phone as we start walking in the direction of Pavlov's Pizza.

Meet me for pizza? I text.

My thumb is still on the send button when the phone rings.

"Is this a joke?" Faye asks me in her usual snap-happy tone.

"Why would I be joking about something like that?" I ask in what even I recognize as a breezy, most un-Louis-ual voice.

"Have you been kidnapped or something?" she asks. "If you have, the code word is Sicilian. Just say Sicilian."

"Stop joking," I say. "I'm serious."

"Pizza. And you're *buying*?"

"Why does everybody keep making such a big deal about that?" I ask.

"Everybody? Louis, there's an *everybody*? Who's everybody?"

"I want you to meet my friend," I say, already knowing pretty much how the next part goes.

There's a lot of loud, clackety, mean, and unnecessary noise on the other end, as my sister drops her phone to the floor and then, I think, kicks it across the kitchen a few times.

I wait, holding the phone away from my ear.

"What happened?" Agatha asks. "Is she still there?"

"Unfortunately, yes," I answer.

"You're telling me you have a *friend*?" my sister calls to me. Sounds like it's from a distance, and that the phone remains on the floor.

"Yes," I growl.

"Pavlov's, right?" she says breathlessly, having picked up the phone now.

She doesn't wait for me to confirm. She hangs up, and I can almost hear her feet beat down the street.

It seems like a long time ago that I thought calling her was such a good idea.

Faye is there before us. "Hi," she says all friendly and energetic, like somebody completely else. She hops up from the booth and waves us toward her. Pavlov's has seating for maybe ten people, so it's not like we would have missed her. But she is truly, frighteningly, happy to see us.

Is she wildly happy for me coming out of my alleged shell here? Or is she reveling in my awkwardness? Either way, I must be even more pathetic than I thought.

"You must be Faye," Agatha says.

"I must be," Faye says.

"I'm Agatha," Agatha says.

Nothing, Louis says.

The three of us slide into the booth, me on one side and them on the other. Faye starts peppering Agatha with questions about how we know each other, and Agatha starts in energetically on the dog-and-frog story that I already know pretty well. I palm-slap the Formica tabletop with both hands—which I figure is some kind of power move that comes with picking up the bill—and stand back up.

Leaning over the table, I say, "Okay, who's having what?"

I don't believe I've ever been in a position to be *this guy* before. Feels pretty good.

"Oh, I already ordered," Faye says. "I hope you don't mind," she adds. To *Agatha*.

"Not at all," Agatha says, waving any lingering concerns out of the air with her hand. "I like everything."

"What?" I say. "Faye, how could you do that? What did you order? Oh right, sausage. It was sausage, wasn't it? I hate the sausage here, and you know that."

"Oh, pull up your pants, Louis," she says, making Agatha giggle. "I ordered a large, half linguica and half *nothing*."

"It's not nothing. A cheese pizza is very much a something. Nothing wrong with it at all."

"Nothing wrong with it at all," Faye repeats.

"Not at all," Agatha adds.

I feel more like my pants *have* fallen down, rather than that I just like cheese pizza. And I'm still standing there leaning over the table.

"I guess I don't need to go up to the counter, then," I say, and start to slide back into my seat.

"Oh, no, you do," Faye says. "They're waiting for you to pay. And we need drinks."

I'm starting to feel quite used and abused. So as Faye and Agatha buddy up, I go to the counter and pay for everything without taking anybody's drink order. We all get Dr Peppers, because I like Dr Pepper.

"And chips," Faye calls out.

I get three bags of chips. Cheese and onion, salt and vinegar, and plain.

After I pay for everything, I return to the table with the chips and drinks. Agatha and Faye have bonded wonderfully in my absence.

"Yes, he is," Faye bleats. "He totally is!"

They both laugh crazy-like as I pass around the Dr Pep-

WALKIN' THE DOG

pers and chips, and I determine that I won't ask what they're referring to. I won't.

I won't.

If anybody has a problem with Dr Pepper or the chip selection, they keep it to themselves. A few minutes later, the pizza completes the ensemble. The three of us swoop down happily onto everything, and the girls don't find the food to be any impediment to conversation at all.

I pick up a slice and direct the arrowhead of it deep into my mouth. There's a stray bit of linguica on it, and it's fantastic. I make a brave, open-minded show of enjoying it.

"So," Faye says, "are you two business partners now?"

There's a lot of food in my mouth at the moment, and I'm struggling mightily to get through it and still maintain my manners but at the same time wrangle this wild beast of a conversation back under control.

I'm chewing fast, as Agatha cheerily and cheekily responds.

"Well," she says, "I haven't received a contract offer yet. But I'd have to seriously consider it if one was on the table."

"It's not," I blurt, and swallow at the same time. And that trick is just as tricky as it sounds.

"Why not?" asks Faye.

That's a good question. It's not a welcome one, since I don't have a good answer handy.

"Oh, he probably doesn't need help," Agatha generously offers.

"He probably does," Faye says. "He's getting, like, new customers by the day."

"Well then, maybe you should be his partner," Agatha says.

Faye and I look at each other silently. Then we both burst out laughing.

"Well, now that that's out of the way," Faye says, "why not Agatha? Is it because she's a girl?"

I haven't had much of a chance to think about it. But maybe it's part of it? Probably not.

"Absolutely not," I say. Convincingly.

"Ha!" Faye says, pointing the last slice of cheese pizza at me like a dagger. "Liar."

There's one more linguica slice lying there, and I'm thinking about it. Until Faye snags it and forces it on Agatha.

"Oh, please, no, I couldn't take the last one," she says.

"Please, take it," I say, hoping this somehow gets me off the hot seat.

Agatha reluctantly agrees to have it. Then not-at-all-reluctantly tears into it with the same savage enthusiasm she brought to each previous slice.

"I know," Faye says, and an actual light bulb may have briefly floated above her wicked head. "Why don't you and I set up our own dog-walking business, Aggie?"

Agatha looks simultaneously nervous and amused, enjoying her pizza and the special brand of Faye chaos—known as Faos—that's bubbling up around us.

"Really?" Agatha asks. "You would want to do that? With me? I'm flattered."

"Don't be flattered," I say. "What are you really up to, Faye?"

She pats her chest with her hand, half closes her eyes, and goes all fluttery and sincere. Therefore, altogether full of crap. "I feel like it's best for everyone. The world needs more female dog walkers. And women-run businesses. We must fight the canine patriarchy."

"Yes," Agatha says with a fist pump.

"Fight the *what*?" I say. "That's not even a thing. How can you fight a thing that's not even a thing?"

Faye reaches across the table and pats my hand, just in case she hasn't already driven me full-on demented. "There'll be plenty of dogs to go around," she says. She turns to Agatha. "We should go, partner. We have organizing to do. Whaddya think, flyers? I think flyers."

Faye bounces up and Agatha starts sliding out behind her. "We can still be friends, right?" she says to me.

She doesn't even wait for an answer, so I'm doubting the sincerity of the whole question.

Flyers. I bought pizza for these people.

4. Live Free or Die

I wish you went," she says. "To the protest."

"Ma!" I say, snapping upright the way a jack-in-the-box must get out of bed. It's the mid-part of middle night that I rarely see.

"Shhh," she says softly, in her old-time, all-time way. She's sitting on the side of my bed. Her hand pushes, just, on my shoulder and I'm back-flat again. She could shush a volcano to calm itself.

"You're home," I say.

"I'm home," she says.

"For good?" I say.

"For good," she says.

My heart races, shush or no. Not even Ma can shush a heart.

"Why didn't you go?" she asks. "To the protest. Like I wanted you to."

Like she wanted me to. She didn't have to say that part. Didn't have to add that.

"I was walkin' the dogs, Ma."

"There's a *g* there," she says.

"Where?"

"At the end of the word 'walking.' Have I been gone long enough that you're a 'deze,' 'dem,' and 'doze' kid now, Louis? Don't be a deze, dem, and doze kid."

"I was walking the dogs, Ma."

"Better. But you still could have been at that protest. It was important, and you could have made a difference."

I must be really tired because I say, "No, I couldn't."

"What did you say?"

"I said I couldn't have made a difference, Ma. That plane was taking off whether I was shouting at it or not. And my way, at least a couple of dogs were happy to see me. And they got healthy exercise."

I will not add that I also made a little spending money. I will not.

"And you made a little money," she says, tilting slightly back, as if she's trying to get a better look at who she's talking to. Or to get farther away from him. Both, probably.

"Um, yeah, I did. But the real protesters did just fine without me, I'm sure."

"You think? Well, I caught it all on the news, and it seemed to me otherwise. And I heard that blowhard mayor going on about what did or did not happen. 'Mistakes were made,' he said; 'Lessons were learned,' he said; 'Blah-blahs were blahed' . . ."

By this time, Ma appears to be rapidly running out of battery. Her voice gets raspier. She stands up, but not quite all the way. There's an arc to her, appearing to magnetically draw her toward the floor.

"It may give you some consolation—though it gives me none—that *one* of my sons did make it to the protest," she says, and if she spoke the words any more wearily, she'd be talking backward.

"Ike?" I hack. "*Ike* was there? As in, my brother, Isaac?"

"The very same," she says.

"But . . . it gives you no consolation, you said. Did he do something? What did he do? Did he upset you?"

She inhales deeply, then does not exhale for a freakish amount of time, feels like a half hour. When she finally lets her breath out again, it feels like a tiny fraction of what she breathed in. Doesn't feel right, or healthy, at all. "I love your brother," she says wearily. "I really do."

Such a lovely sentiment, and it also feels like the worst possible start to whatever she needs to say.

"Ah, for fuck's sake, Ma," I snap.

"Louis," she gasps, and it's a real gasp of a gasp.

I shouldn't have said it, shouldn't have done that at all. She obviously did not have an extra gasp to spend, and I was wrong to take it from her. "I'm sorry, Ma, it just came out."

"There was . . . violence," she says, visibly shuddering. "And he wouldn't even have known about it if I hadn't brought it up at dinner. He was like some kind of storm trooper; they all were. 'Security' detail, the news called them. I don't see how anybody could feel secure with that. . . . I was so ashamed when I realized . . ."

My blood boils. But enough already. She can't take this now.

She's staring straight down now, and I worry that she could topple over.

"Maybe we should talk about it in the morning," I suggest.

"That would be good," she says in a hoarse whisper. She stands, a bit unsteadily. "Good night, son," she says, and withdraws.

I stare at her shadowy absence for several seconds before allowing my eyes to close again.

In the morning I bounce out of bed with at least a couple of kinds of conflicted, nervous energy. I'm excited to see Ma but at the same time anxious about the Ike thing. I've half convinced myself that I dreamed it and she never spoke the words. I'm dressed and down the hall so fast I may in fact be still unconscious when I find Dad in the kitchen on the phone. He's hardly ever on the phone. He's pacing, agitated, flustered, none of which is a regular feature of Dadism.

"Where's Ma?" I ask.

He stops mid-pace and stares at me. There's a small voice still going on the other end of the phone when he demands of me, "Why did you ask that?"

"Because she said we'd talk this morning. She came in to see me last night."

Dad gives me a dumbfounded stare. Then the voice on the phone gets noticeably more insistent, and he returns to it. "The truth is, I can't tell you for sure now whether we've seen her or not. I can tell you that *I* haven't seen her. Let me talk to my family and get back to you. Okay? All right, I'll call you back."

He hangs up and resumes staring at me.

"Who was that?" I ask.

"It was the hospital—"

"The Knoll."

"Yeah. Your mother left there sometime between dinner last night and breakfast this morning. They have no idea where she's gone to."

"Here, Dad. She's gone here. I told you, she came into my room. We talked. It was great just to see her. Weird, but great. Did you not see her? How did you not see her? Where did she sleep?"

I'm suddenly in a panic I didn't see coming. I'm running around the house, checking every room and every corner, as if Dad could have somehow missed her. It's not a big house.

"I don't know where she slept," he says, "but it wasn't here."

I walk into Faye's room without knocking, which is bad form and dangerous.

"Did you see her?" I ask.

She's deep under the covers and sounds asleep when she says, "I'm only gonna ask this to help me decide whether to kill you. Did I see who?"

"Ma," I snap, like it's such an obvious answer.

Faye jumps up. "Here? Ma's here?"

"No," Dad says.

"Yes," I say. "Or she was. Last night. But now she's not here. She's not anywhere, apparently."

Dad's phone rings, and he takes the call down the hall.

"Is everybody going crazy now just because you had another *dream*, Louis?"

"It was *not* a dream," I say.

"There's no shame in it," she says. "I dream about her too. The difference is, I wake up eventually."

"Stop it, Faye," I say, and follow Dad's voice back to the kitchen.

"Oh, thank god, Eleanor," Dad says, and he sounds like the air being drained out of a monster truck tire.

Eleanor is the day manager at the shelter, A Woman's Place, where Ma's the night manager.

"I understand," Dad says. "I'll be right down. I'll take her . . . wherever she wants to go. Here, the Knoll, wherever. Thank you, thank you . . . ," he says, and he's still thanking her as he hangs up.

"She went to *work*?" says Faye, who walked up behind me at some point.

"Not to work, exactly," Dad says. "But yeah, there. She went to the shelter. Eleanor says they could make space for her for just the one night. They're overrun as it is, with women who really need to be there. Your mom doesn't really need to be there, and so they have to have the space for those who do. Nobody understands that better than Mom."

He slips into calling her "Mom" when he's at his mushiest.

"So where does she need to be, Dad?" I ask like a little kid. "Here, right? You're bringing her home."

Dad is suddenly rushed and flushed, heading for the door. "Eleanor thinks she needs to be back at the Knoll," he says, sounding like somebody trying to sound strong. "But she doesn't have to be anywhere in particular. It's all up to her. I'm going to find out where she wants to go, and I will take her there. She took off from the Knoll for a reason. Something set her off, and so she needs to be sorted out again before she can settle anywhere."

The silence that floods the house after he slams the door on those words is suffocating. Faye pats my back medium hard and retreats to her room. I stand right where I am and retreat to nowhere.

It takes probably ten minutes before I figure out what to do with myself.

I'm at Faye's door. This time I wisely knock on it. She tells me to come in, and I find her sitting at her desk. She's leaning hard into her computer screen, and her work.

"Is that what I think it is?" I ask.

"I don't like to presume too much about what you think," she says.

"Is it a flyer for your new business?"

She stares at her work on the screen. There's some deliberately primitive artwork (my sister doesn't do accidental anything) of two girl-types walking along, holding leashes with dozens of very daffy-happy dogs attached. The artwork is like from the Mr. Men/Little Miss books.

"Oh, I don't know," she says wearily. "I don't know. I don't care. I don't know."

"Well," I say, "that's a lot of 'I don't, I don't' . . . from somebody who just went to the trouble of stealing both my business and my new friend."

She sighs heavily, then swings her desk chair back around in my direction.

"I didn't steal either of those things, Louis, honestly. Like I said before, there are plenty of dogs to go around—if we even want them, since we really only need a few. And frankly, there is enough Aggie to go around too. She really, *really* could use some friends. She's worse than you."

"What's that supposed to mean?"

"It means, you could use some friends."

"No, I couldn't."

"There ya go."

"Anyway, this all serves you right. I *had* a friend, and you went and stole her. Then you got tired of her right away and so now you're talking about Aggie and me like *we're* the problems, when everything was fine until you came along."

She pauses.

"Okay, take her back, then," she says. "I already have plenty of friends anyway."

"Frankly, I don't see how that's possible either."

We have a thing we do, Faye and me. Don't quite know when we worked it out, or how. It just came about naturally, without our ever talking it through. What we do is, we'll have a conversation that is actually two or more conversations, about something or nothing, but not about what maybe we mean to be talking about. It can sound like we don't even hear each other, the way we bypass questions and comments and just jump to whatever question or comment comes into our heads next.

"Thank you for the pizza," Faye says.

"You don't really want to walk dogs," I say.

"Agatha promised to teach me harmonica," she says. "I think that'll be cool. You wanna learn?"

"Only a month left until I'm off to real school," I say. "Are you gonna miss having me around?"

"I think we should start having more breakfast foods for supper. Bacon and eggs, pancakes . . . Just to change stuff up, y'know?"

"Don't you feel like it's not even summer right now? Like it hasn't been summer all summer?"

"Also, if we start doing supper stuff for breakfast as well as breakfast stuff for supper, we can finally answer the question of which came first, the chicken or the egg. Because we'll decide, depending on the day. Cool, huh?"

"I wish I went to the protest like Ma wanted me to. I should have gone. I don't know why I didn't."

"This mean we're talking about Ma now?" she asks.

"It does not," I say.

"Well, sure, let's talk about something altogether unrelated. Have you seen it yet?"

"Which 'it' is that?"

"The 'it' your mother asked you to go to, which you

managed not to do, and because nature abhors a vacuum, the *anti-you* went in your place."

"So, that actually did happen, then," I say.

She spins her chair back around and addresses her computer.

As she searches for the offending video, she narrates a bit. "They say the protest was 'infiltrated' by thugs. But they also say there is speculation that these guys were supposed security for the mayor, paid to show up." She looks up at me over her shoulder. "Y'know, kinda the same rationale you had for *not* being there. Huh, coincidence, or what? You're both employed by dogs."

"Faye, I can already tell this is gonna hurt enough without the evil commentary, so, please? I know for pretty certain that this is the thing that pushed Ma over the edge. Ike did it to her."

"Yeah, right," she says, "it is . . ." She hits play and leans back. "Ike gotta Ike, huh?"

Sure enough, we're both right. It hurts. Even if I didn't know anybody in this clip, it would hurt to watch how the people were treated when they were just trying to stick up for some folks who needed help. Chants were chanted, signs were waved, but not a lot of anything appeared to be happening until the 'security' showed up. And Ike was, as Ike is, flamboyant and conspicuous by his bigness of presence. He and his pals were physical from the get-go, shoving people to the ground and shouting like human bullhorns at them once they were down. The stuff they did looked vicious to me, but it fell just short of what I'd call brutality. It also fell short of human decency.

Almost as if they'd been trained to go just so far.

A wave of true sickness rises up in me. Not at the spectacle of malice before my eyes. But at my imagining of my mother watching this. A vomit tide reaches my Adam's apple.

"Turn it off, Faye," I croak.

She does.

"Sure you don't wanna talk about Ma instead?" she says.

"Pretty sure we just did," I say.

The doorbell rings.

"Excellent," I say, trotting off to answer it.

I throw open the door to find Agatha standing there.

"This is a surprise," I say.

"Not to me, it isn't," she says.

I hear the printer start cranking up in Faye's room.

"You expecting Aggie?" I call.

"Yup," she calls back.

I wave Agatha into the house and follow her down the hall toward my sister's room. She's playing the harmonica as she walks. Sounds like a square dance.

Faye pops out her door just as we get there. She's got a fistful of papers.

"They're ready?" Aggie says excitedly. She plays the train-chug tune as she looks at a flyer.

"Wonderful," Aggie says.

"We're going to deliver flyers through people's mail slots," Faye says to me. "You wanna come?"

Agatha turns my way. "Oh, please come, Louis," she pleads. She appears to mean it. Weirdly, so does Faye.

"Jeez, it sounds like fun," I say, "putting me out of business and all. But I think I'll wait here for Dad to come home."

Faye gently pats one of my arms on the way past, because she knows. Agatha pats the other, because she's Agatha.

5. Sight Unseen

It isn't really a shock when Dad returns Ma-less a couple of hours later. It's just past lunchtime. She's back at the Knoll, and he stayed with her long enough to conclude that she was fine now.

If she's fine, why isn't she *here*? Fine is *here*. *Here* is fine. When she's fine, she's here. When she's not fine, she's *there*.

She can't stay there forever, can she? She could just appear here unannounced again, right? It's like when you're waiting for a package to arrive. You don't want to go anywhere. In case you miss it. I don't want to go anywhere.

Not quite a people person to begin with, I have to confess that the whole Ma-visit-or-maybe-not thing has me wondering about going out at all. I have no idea how much of it is logic and how much is dream-hope, but I have this sense that she's about to come home any minute and I need to be here for that.

I'm probably not very good at appearing to be loitering without intent.

"Don't you have a new doggo gig starting today?" Faye says.

I do. She's right. She's 100 percent always right.

"No," I say.

She walks to the calendar hanging off the side of the fridge. It's a cat calendar, which, I don't even know what it's doing in this house. I'm allergic to cat calendars.

"Says here ya do," says she.

"Can't believe anything cats say," I say.

"Well, this cat has your handwriting."

I don't want to confess to just being weird and waiting for Ma to return.

"I'm not well enough," I say. "My noggin's kinda throbbin', and my stomach's getting pukey."

"Okay," she says brightly, "I'll go do it for you. I could use the money, and another new client."

In the area of credit where credit's due, my sister is the bank president. She knows what she's doing. And right now, what she's doing is provoking me with her knowledge that I'm not going to simply let her walk off with my money. Unless I'm somewhere much nearer to death than I currently am.

In the network of mountain caves and tunnels that make up her mind, she's doing all this for my own good.

I know this.

I hate her for this.

"No," I say. Defiantly, as far as I can tell.

"No?" she says, and waits for the rest.

I wait along with her. Nothing much is forthcoming. Until.

The house trembles with the approach of the beastly Harley and its beastly rider.

Faye and I stare at each other. Her face is as blank as my mind is, so at least we're on the same page. The sound of the bike cutting out in the driveway is as alarming as the sound of the engine was in the first place.

I have a most unusual feeling: a feeling that *something must be done. By me.*

The original equipment part of my brain thinks about bolting for the back door as he undoubtedly approaches the front. Rocks and hard places rarely get together with such a perfect *click* as this. I do the only sensible thing and freeze rigid between them, right in the middle of the kitchen.

But there's a new modification to that brain. It was bolted on when I saw Ma's face as she described her Ike-induced heartbreak, in that crackled voice last night.

Make no mistake, I don't love this new addition. I far prefer the *run away* bit.

The front door opens, and big Ike bellows, "Anybody home?"

Faye takes my hand. "What are you thinking?" she asks, looking both concerned and amused at my undoubtedly fragmented expression.

"I haven't the slightest idea."

"Are you going to, like, confront him, Louis? I mean, your face, your eyes . . . If you were anybody else, I would say you look like you're spoiling for a fight. But you're you."

My head nods itself somehow. It's the only part of me

capable of movement. Previous me would have fled by now. Current me remains bolted to the floor. Idiot current me.

"I could at least get you outside, if you can't do it yourself," she says. "Unlike you, I can smack him without consequences. Maybe you should just run, live to fight another day?"

"Excellent. Then I'd just have to wait around for *that* horrifying day."

I shake my head, but since I'm looking over her shoulder at Ike walking into the room, it's entirely possible I'm reacting to the reality of him rather than her generous offer.

"No, Faye," I say with shocking certainty. "I have to do this."

"Do *what?*" she says with what looks like the vanishingly rare thing, a Faye panic.

"Louis," he says, pronouncing it Lou-ee because I don't like it like that.

"Isaac," I respond, because he doesn't like that, either.

He just grins at me, very toothy. "I-K-E." He says each letter firmly.

"That's pronounced 'Icky,'" Faye says to me with a spectacular sort of phony helpful sincerity. I do so love it when she's on my side of the net.

Ike brushes past her in order to lay a freakishly genuine-feeling hug on me.

"How you holding up?" he says, leaning back and rapping my skull with his knucky-knucks.

I nearly fall backward onto the floor, but he grabs me quick, pulls me close to him again.

"Yikes," he says. "You need to be more careful, little man."

It's almost impossible to tell what he means by that, because it could mean a thousand things. It's probably *supposed* to mean a thousand things.

I don't understand. But that's nothing new.

Faye shoulder-bumps Ike aside, like he did to her. She tries to bundle me in the direction of the back door.

"No," I say, working my way around her to get right up close to Ike.

"What did you do?" I ask shakily. Then, as if I fear he will answer, I unleash a cascade of questions. "Why did you have to be so cruel? Did you know you were being filmed? Of course you knew. Did you just go to the protest because you heard about it from Ma? Is that where you get your insider info? From Ma? That's sick, Ike. That's really sick."

He goes so calm and still with me, it's like an insult. As is the inevitable smile. There it is.

I shove him hard in the chest with both hands.

He does me the added insult of not moving backward an inch. Faye rushes between us.

"I didn't realize you cared so much," he says over her shoulder. "Otherwise, you woulda, like, been there."

I reach over Faye's shoulder, and I slap Ike right in the face.

I know it's the single stupidest thing I've ever done. Not wrong, though.

Faye spins right around to grab me and keep Ike at her back.

"Are you out of your mind?" she says. "He'll mop the floor with you."

"Let him," I snarl.

"Y'know," she says, as sweetly as possible, "I'm not sure you understand how beatings work. They're not like mopping at all."

In a lot of ways, Faye is as strong as Ike, or stronger. Mentally, psychologically, she's got him beat.

But then, there's the strength of good ol' physical strength.

He walks through her like she's standing water.

It's a Faye sandwich, as she tries to defend me. But he has the three of us squeezed together. His iron-claw hand is clamped around the back of my head. He's pulling us all together, and it might even be heartwarming if it wasn't so threatening.

All three of our heads, cheek-to-cheek-to-cheekbones, are pressed together, as he delivers it: "You will never get away with that again, little man. This is love, my not killing you. Enjoy it now. I don't know how much more of that kind of love I have."

I break out of Faye's grip and launch myself at Ike. "Do you even think about Ma when you do stuff like that?" is the last thing I say before I can't say any more. He seizes me in a headlock so viselike it muffles my voice, loosens some teeth, and makes breathing a full-time job.

"You do make me laugh, little boy. And it's a good thing, too. You need to cool your jets now, and it'll be okay later. I'll forget all this ever happened, and you'll be forgiven. I'm good like that."

I do manage to growl. Unsurprisingly, it doesn't accomplish much.

"Faye, you're the smart one," he says. "You do the right thing and get him outta here before anything bad happens."

I think Faye is genuinely concerned for my well-being. She practically assumes control of the headlock as she comes over to take custody of me.

"You sure you don't want me to come with?" she whispers as she shuffles me to the back door.

"I'm sure," I say. "But if he tries to follow me, I want you to tackle him."

Faye, at approximately one-third of Ike's size, is probably the only person I would ask to do that. And definitely the only one I'd expect to succeed at it.

"Done," she says, shoving me out the back door.

Done, and I run.

Fortunately, there are always dogs to run to. And happy customers talk to each other at a rate faster than any flyers can reach them. I have a new gig, and even though I'm a half hour early, my job allows me to look more conscientious than neurotic as I flee my homicidal brother.

"Introductory special," I jabber at the befuddled dog mother as she hands me the keys to the canines. "Bonus thirty minutes of walking, on the house."

There's a semicircular road that runs up a high hill on the inland side of our town. Once you turn off the main street and head down into the short valley approaching the hill, it all gets a little bit farmy before it gets a lot foresty. It's a good day for me to be on this particular trek, calm and quiet as it is. Mostly what you ever run into on this route is the odd cyclist or three, a jogger here or there who passes you by with an *I'm too busy and sweaty* grunt and a wave. Kinda perfect.

These dogs' parents—and whoo-boy do my hackles rise when they insist that that's who they are—were adamant that their two little ones needed a long midday constitutional, and they needed me to do it because all four of them were suffering daily intestinal, and emotional, distress all at the same time.

Which is why I'm now out on the semicircular, semi-rural walk with the border terriers, Jekyll and Hyde. Their names don't make a lot of sense, since they both behave exactly the same as each other. Though maybe we'll test that, since we're walking at the highest possible noon on the sunniest possible day.

Even though the terriers have a comforting, medium-fast trotting style, and neither one of them is a homicidal maniac like the Mr. Hyde of legend, I still find myself looking around kind of edgy-like as we stroll. I wave at the cyclists—who don't wave back because they're Lycra-slimed jerks—and I grunt at the already-grunting joggers. But relaxation still escapes me.

My mother was gone. Then she was back. Maybe. Then she was gone again.

I can do better, though. I can and I will. Jekyll and Hyde and I will change things back to normal, right here, right now.

We make our way all the way down the valley and bang the left turn that will have us climbing the steepest hill in town. We cross over the small bridge crossing the small stream, and when the incline grows quickly tougher, I find myself happy for that. My small pals, being terriers after all, like nothing more than a challenge. They chug faster up the hill than they did on the downslope. Things are improving. The sun is lashing us, and that too feels like a blessing. Sometimes, I think, the world needs to demand stuff from you before you can come up with *the stuff* that the world needs to see.

The road slices through a couple of farms, or one bisected farm, anyway. Cattle graze on the downhill slope to our left, sheep and horses on the uphill to our right. I'm gradually easing into it, feeling somewhat healthier from the blossoming suntan that seems to be washing my headache out of the way. I've almost had enough of the searing sunshine when we crest the hill, and the wide openness is switched out for the sudden drop of a lush tunnel of greenery that folds over us and the country road we're navigating.

The temperature changes instantly, lowering several degrees. The light shifts, going shady-sweet in a way that makes my eyes feel altogether superior to my regular eyes. Like I got a transplant from a hawk or an owl. The thick green moisture of this air is so real I find myself feeling it with my fingertips the way you would with silk or velvet.

Jekyll, Hyde, and I keep on marching our way up this hill.

It's very close to bliss. Until we come across a monster turd planted right in the middle of the road.

Having picked up about three hundred of these by now, I'm not quite immune to the mankiness of the task. But I do consider it to be part of the deal that comes with having a dog. Or walking one for someone else and their money.

So I hate it when other people don't pick up after their dogs. *Hate* it.

You might think, hey, you've picked up one crap, you've picked up all of 'em.

That would be very wrong thinking on your part.

Not sure why it should *be*, or even that it *should* be, but it is very different to be picking up a load belonging to some mutt that's not your responsibility from one that is. I did that once, by accident. A dog I was walking left a deposit in some long grass on the edge of the soccer field, and when I went to do the right thing by it, I picked up . . . some *other* crap. It was not fresh.

I know, none of them are fresh. They're never fresh.

But this one was old and cold, mushy like leftover oatmeal. I was instantly horrified, but couldn't stop what I was doing because, ugh, I was doing it, wasn't I? I practically ralphed three times on my way to the doo-posit box. Then I had to go back and collect the one I was aiming for in the first place. That one was new and warm and solid, but that was not as comforting as it sounds, and still, the damage to me was done and I nearly honked again.

That moment, for me, was significant. Like when Batman's parents were killed. Nothing was ever the same again. *I was never the same again.*

It's one of the true crimes against humanity to leave a steaming lump on a public pathway, and as I've gotten immersed in the dog-care world, I've taken this increasingly personally. I feel my whole head go hot and bubbly like a bag of microwave soup every time I come across one in my travels. I feel it, as an insult, to *me*.

I know it says something about me when I declare that if I came across a murderer murdering someone, and at the same time he allowed his dog to take a squat without cleaning up after him, I'd hate that person more about the dump than about the homicide.

The lump of turd is what has me beside myself.

I wish I was beside myself, so both of me could hunt down the person responsible for this atrocity.

However, it's just me here, and I simply cannot pick up another dog's befoulment.

Because I am me, and Jekyll and Hyde are them, we just swerve around the mess and keep walking. Suddenly, in the distance, before the hill crests, something bounds across the road. Since these dogs are thrilled and engaged by everything, they're thrilled and engaged. They strain and growl and yank me along.

I follow enthusiastically, because the bounding something looks unusual, strange and oddly elegant, like a skinny white wolf with an odd, awkward gait.

Tremendously long, gangly legs. All three of them.

When we travel another twenty yards, the dogs and I see it again, galloping back across the road in the opposite direction.

As we get closer, it performs the same dash, back and forth and back again, apparently heedless of our presence. Except, almost inviting us to look and see.

It stops, near the side of the road, on the right, just before the woods begin. I think it's a dog, though I've never seen anything quite like it. It's brilliant white, blinding, bleachy white. It's allowing us to get closer, and as we do, I'm thinking there's something like a big greyhound here, but with a wild, ropy coat of hair draped over its back. And then, the missing leg. It's the left front.

I've seen a few three-legged dogs in my time, but, wow. Because of the build of this creature—kind of like a sunfish in the way it's huge from the side view but flat from head-on—the missing leg is unignorable. It's like it was sheared off right at the shoulder, and you could sell advertising on the side of this dog, like a hairy billboard.

Billie. It takes me three nanoseconds to decide this is Billie.

She surprises me by standing entirely still as Jekyll, Hyde, and I bring our fascination right up close to her. She has an odd serenity about her, as the terriers don't ruffle her at all. Her eyes are not huge, but there's something about them that makes them seem really big. And they look right, deep, into you. Or into me, anyway.

They're very pretty eyes, though she's not a pretty dog. She seems like she's wearing makeup. She makes me sad, and I don't even understand why.

Billie allows me to stroke her streamlined head, and she

allows J&H to orbit her and sniff her out every which way. I look all around for any sign of owners or walkers or some connection between her and the human community. There are no signs. She has no collar. She seems at home with having no home.

We continue our walk, and Billie joins us. The dogs all get along, and I'm made stupid happy by this. There are ten minutes between our finding Billie and the point where the woodsy hill becomes edge-of-town housing again. As if there's one of those invisible electric fences, Billie stops when the woods stop. She pauses, causing us to halt. We look back, she blinks in our direction, and then she bounds back into the woods.

I watch her go, and something, something ridiculous, makes my heart claw at itself. Jekyll and Hyde may miss her too, but if they do, it passes quickly, and they get on with their merrier-terrier lives.

6. Low Profile

IS IT NORMAL TO BE WORRIED BECAUSE THINGS ARE GOING well? I mean, the demands of the dog-care business, at which I'm suddenly very successful. Word spreads like crazy once you get a reputation as a reliable and reasonably priced mutt-minder, and that's the reputation I've rapidly gathered around myself. And if I may blow my own muzzle here, I have managed to see off all unnamed annoying girl challengers to my crown with hardly any noticeable drop-off in my business.

It's already gotten so good, I can see myself doing this forever, and who needs homeschooling, or anyschooling, for that matter? I'm making money, and money is making *me*. See what I did there? I was never that snappy before. It's gotta be the money.

But there I went and did something else, too. The school thing. I don't know who I'm pep-talking with all this, but nobody who matters, that's for sure. I can hear the huffing breath of my new school life right on my neck now, and even money isn't gonna alter that scenario.

But for the time being, the last weeks of summer, all I need is a way with dogs—check—and an even greater way with their owners—check—and I'm cleaning up.

Yes, it also involves a whole lot of cleaning up. But you get used to it. Just like you get used to all the pet owners and their quirks. And the undead hours. If you're gonna be doing this job, you'll often find yourself patrolling the landscape before dawn and after dusk.

The midday walks are overrun with other canine beasts and their walker beasts. Rotten with them.

Me, I'll take the fringe hours, and the quiet, anytime. Give me a sunrise or a sunset, a pack o' pups and some landscape all to ourselves, and I'm happy as your proverbial pig-in-poop. Other people tend to just mean trouble.

There are four dachshunds that I'm required to walk at the least sociable hours. They've been banned from the dog parks altogether, in fact, because of their sinister behavior. Their names are Ace, King, Queen, and Jack. Their owner, another neighbor of Old Man Dan's, says he won them in a card game. I don't believe him because from what I understand—meaning Dad told me—you shouldn't believe a word that comes out of the mouth of a gambler. The dogs don't answer to anything at all, so I guess he can call them what he wants.

Three mornings a week, I have to collect them from the place. They live in the garage, and I almost never see the guy, Mr. Basset, or anybody else at that hour. That hour being six a.m., or sometimes even earlier. I have a map of the neighborhood that he printed out and marked up with several different highlighters indicating by colors red, yellow, and green, which streets I'm supposed to always avoid, or avoid if I can, or sure, go for it.

I think Basset stole the sausages. That would explain his insistence on keeping an even lower profile than the three-inch ground clearance they already manage.

This is the fourth time. I walked the gang-of-four three times last week, and now we're starting again. They're an odd bunch in that they haven't given me any guff from day one, while at the same time they haven't quite embraced me either.

Ha. I have to laugh. And I do. The idea of these characters embracing anything, with those tiny arms of theirs. Priceless. I was so fascinated by the second time out that I was completely obsessed with trying to count their countless little steps as we walked along the road. It's like walking long, hairy hummingbirds. I got dizzy trying and had to sit on the curb. They hardly noticed. Just fluttered around and around me until I got back up.

There are a lot of trees in this town of ours. But they mostly don't all clump together, into something like a woods. I admire that about our trees. They're not needy.

We go left out of Basset's driveway and encounter our first clump of about a dozen spruces, a hundred yards up on the opposite side of the road. We cross, as we do, so each of the dogs can pee on or around each of the trees, as they do. Mission accomplished, we recross and follow the road, a gently winding couple hundred more yards to the next clump of trees. My swarm descends, pees are wee'd, and we trundle on. Not the loveliest of walks around these parts, but it is fairly secluded, the dogs clearly enjoy it, and it's what the boss tells me to do.

It's one of those great mysteries of capitalism my mother conveniently forgot to include in my lessons: do exactly what people ask you to do, and they'll give you money for it. She won't be happy when she finds out I found out.

We reach a modest little cemetery, maybe fifty souls deep, and we enter. It's square and boxed in on three sides with a crumbling drystone wall. Some classy rubble around the fourth side hints at a church that was probably here a long time ago. The sausages can wriggle riot in here while I examine the modest headstones. None of them come up higher than my thigh; there are no skulls or angels or sing-songy prayer-poems to complicate things. Just names and dates carved so plainly into granite that they seem almost embarrassed to have bothered anybody with their passings. First member of this club appears to have dropped in about two hundred years ago, with the most recent coming to rest around Korean War time.

It takes a special request to get them to open up a plot here for anybody today. Ma's indicated she might like to do that. I've indicated I might like to not hear that. But since it was just part of a larger unwelcome conversation about how she'd sourced a lovely wicker casket . . . because "why should the worms have to work any harder to get at me? They do enough for everybody, the poor things." I had my hands full enough reminding her she was nowhere near death, never mind discussing final resting places and the paperwork required to get into them.

She is nowhere near death. Nowhere.

Unlike myself and the suddenly unleashed sausage dogs now. I love a cemetery. Cemeteries *deserve* love, more than almost anywhere else. They earn it. I don't know anybody in this graveyard, but as I weave among the stones and read among the names, I suddenly feel as if I do. Is that what happens to everybody when they pass through one of these places? Do they feel for these people they never knew when otherwise, why should we care?

Or do we somehow bring our own people in here with us?

The dogs have no respect. They're disrespecting all over, like a rude little plague. I can't have this, and I maybe handle them a tiny bit too roughly as I wrangle them back onto the leashes.

I drag them back to the twisty road, past a tree here, a blank billboard there, a van that looks like it's been parked in the same spot since before I was born.

Some dog walks are lovely. Some don't need to be. Some shouldn't be.

Our destination is a largely abandoned industrial park with cracking, bubbling, weed-rich asphalt sprawling front and back. I can't think of a single noncriminal activity that would render this place attractive to anybody, but it's the must-do place on the sausage itinerary. There's even a big orange North Star of an asterisk drawn on the color-coded cheat sheet of our journey. It's as if it's the showstopper finale on one of those Hollywood maps of the stars' homes.

And, well, for reasons known to themselves, the dogs go ape for the place. They strain like a minuscule mule team as soon as we get close. They pull me with all their might—a shocking amount of might, to give them fair dues—until we're around to the Wild West of the rear lot, where I let them loose. There's a natural amphitheater sort of arrangement here, as the lot spills out across a football field of disintegrating pavement until it bumps to a spontaneous finish at a great mound of dirty, dusty hill at the far end.

The whole herd of them fly across the lot straight toward the base of the hill. I can't tell what's got their attention, but they're making quite a ruckus, dashing to one spot, then another, then another, yelping and digging and bumping and trampling one another.

I figure I should go over there and look in on them. But who cares, with as much fun as they appear to be having? No rush.

I'm halfway to the hill when a something zooms past, jolting me sideways. It's a great, speeding hairy machine of a thing, looking like one of those desert-land-speed-record-attempt rockets. I stare, agog at first, until I compute that the brute missile is heat-seeking directly toward my tiny responsibilities. I start running.

A few strides in, I become aware that I'm not running

alone. Somebody's chugging along beside me. The guy's probably a couple of years older than me.

"It's the rats," he says.

"What's the rats?" I ask.

"Getting the dogs all worked up. They love it down there. The base of the hill is like a rodent apartment building. Holes, tunnels, in and out all over. That'll be what your dogs are after."

I feel somehow insulted. Like somehow only my dogs are rat-tastic.

"And yours," I snort.

"No," he says.

"No?" I say.

"No," he says. "My dog's after your dogs."

I'm not particularly fast, but I suddenly get a burst of blast and leave the kid snorting my exhaust. I hear him laughing back there and realize he's just had a burst of *who cares?*

He's still laughing when I reach the scene and start trying to break things up. It's a lot of work. There's snarling and screeching and no small amount of biting going on. The other dog is a Rottweilerian muscle mound, one who obviously has history, judging by the leather executioner's mask he has on.

As I get more desperate and the sausages get more chaotic (and I assume the rats kick back for a bit), the kid laughs that much harder. At first I think he's just sadistic. Then I gather myself up enough to realize what's really going on.

The sausages rule.

They're absolutely tormenting the Rottweiler. Two of them are dangling from either side of his head like a vicious pair of earrings. The other two are doing pure evil. They're clearly, deliberately, focusing all their energy—and teeth—on the big guy's . . . arrangement of private equipment. One is working from the forward undercarriage while the other dirty devil goes after it from the southern cross. I can barely watch as the back-seat assassin does that killer canine thing of champing down on the prey and shaking it maniacally back and forth and all around in the ultimate kill shot.

I don't honestly know what the greater horror is here, what these bitty savages can do or how funny the other kid is still finding it.

"It's extra funny," he says, "because my dog drops turds the exact same size and shape and color as your dogs, but they can still beat him up. It's like, revenge of the angry butt biscuits."

Eventually he helps me, and we separate the little ones from the big one. It's like the sausages are sprouting, gremlin-style, right out of the big dog's fur.

You know how some kids will agree to have a fight, meet up someplace, and then they're done with it in like three minutes? This is kind of like that, as the fighters are separated and sprint immediately—together—back to the important business of ratting. It's like there never was any fighting, and they all just carpooled together to get here.

The kid has just about stopped laughing when I finally get a chance to take him in.

"Hey. I know you, don't I?" I say.

It's not even a real question, but that's what you're supposed to say. I know him. He came to us for several weeks last fall as my mom tutored him for the SATs. He's a few grades ahead of me but not all that big. I always thought he looked like one of those great soccer players who have only one name. His name is Cyrus, calls himself Cy. I came up with this gag where every time he'd show up at the house, I'd greet him with this huge, exaggerated sigh. Right, Cy/Sigh, yeah? I liked him a lot, came to look forward to seeing him.

"Uh-huh," he says. "Louis, right?"

"Yes," I say. Then I do the big Cy sigh.

"Still?" he says flatly.

Come to think of it, I did a lot of laughing alone at that joke.

The dogs are playing whack-a-rat with the critters appearing and disappearing at will through their endless network of entrances and exits. The dogs are going mental, but they enjoy mental. Good times all around.

"I really liked your mom," Cy says as we stare off in the same direction toward the action. "How's she doing?"

I sink a little. I come this close to puffing out a great involuntary sigh. I catch it before it can come out all wrong.

I make a move to answer his actual question.

I push down another sigh.

"What's your dog's name?" I ask finally.

"Pierre," he says.

"It wasn't fair, to be fair," I say in a not unzombie voice.

"Huh?" he says.

"Y'know, my dogs beating up your dog? While your dog was muzzled?"

"Oh, right. Well, also to be fair, my dog's a *dog*. Yours are chipmunks. So, kinda evens out."

"S'pose," I say.

Two of the sausages disappear into ratholes. Ten seconds later they both rocket back out, yelping. Cyrus starts laughing again, and I join him now as all the dogs come bounding in the direction of their humans' protective custody.

"I don't remember you having these guys," Cy says, kneeling to greet the returning hairy heroes.

"No," I say. "I'm a professional dog wrangler these days."

He looks up at me, head tilted confused-like.

"Really?" he says. "Your mom allows you to charge for your services? She wouldn't even let me pay her for tutoring. Made me go down and give the money straight to the women's shelter. In person, so I could learn something while I was at it."

Never knowingly not tutoring, my ma.

"I didn't know that," I say. "She's always doing embarrassing stuff like that."

"She's a great lady," he says.

"She is," I just about manage to say out loud.

"I did well in my exams," he says.

I nod, because of course he did.

"I'd like to stop by and tell your mom. Thank her again. If I may. If you think it would be all right."

I think it would be very, very all right.

Or maybe not. I've gotten a lot of things wrong of late. About Ma. About other important life stuff and people stuff that maybe I wouldn't have gotten wrong if I hadn't gotten things about my mother wrong. So I try not to take too much for granted.

I'll check with Ma, about a visit from Cy.

First, it's homeward we're bound.

"Where do you live, anyway?" I ask him as we cross the ghostly garden of the broken parking lot.

"Nowhere," he says. "I'm not telling you."

The sausages are now in love with Pierre. They swim alongside him like pilot fish to a great white shark. Like an entourage to a puffed-up celebrity. Like bishops to a pope.

Pierre glances up toward me and does a scary one-side snarl. I could swear he's hearing my thoughts. *I am not a pope,* is what I'm sure he's saying.

"Nowhere *and* you're not telling me? Cy, those are two different answers."

Cy half turns, gives me the same exact look and sound his hound just did. "You want a third?" he asks.

"No," I say. "I'm pretty sure I just got one, thanks."

The bunch of us make our way back down the winding, empty road we traveled earlier to get to the sausages' happy place. Cy and I speak less than the dogs do, but the stroll passes pleasantly enough. Eventually and almost wordlessly, Cy and his dog break away from us and cross over the street. They are approaching a dusty and scarred old apartment complex that

I have seen many times but have never taken much notice of. It always looks as abandoned as the industrial wasteland where the dogs and rats love to play.

I can't believe Cy or anybody else still lives there. I have quickly learned not to over-ask. I'm not untrainable.

"I'll see ya, Lou," he says without looking back.

Nobody has ever called me Lou.

"See ya soon, Cy," I say. And I know I will.

7. Flying Fish

IF MA'S APPEARANCE AT MY BEDSIDE FELT LIKE SOME KIND of fever dream, what am I to make of this?

"Hey, Dad," I say after following unfamiliar sounds and finding him lying on his bed, dressed to go out for work but obviously not doing so despite the relative lateness of the hour. He's getting a late start, lying there listening to the radio. This is not a thing that happens casually.

"Hey, Louis," he says evenly. As if everything is just as it should be.

"Are you okay?" I ask.

He starts feeling himself up. It's not as icky as it sounds, and makes me laugh a little. "Far as I can tell, the answer's yes," he says.

"Taking the day off, then?" I ask hopefully.

I like my father being around.

I like my father.

"Just this portion of it," he says. "I have a booking later, to take some guys out fishing for blues. They're running like mad right now. Bluefish season is like Christmas for me. Best of the best days of the year."

"I know, Dad," I say. Ma is crazy for bluefish, is what this is about. It's the only thing with a central nervous system she will eat, because she can't help herself. She tried to give it up last year at this time. Didn't work out. Dad had to live on the boat practically the whole month of August because the situation grouched her up so badly. She said he looked and smelled like a big fat bluefish every day when he came home, and she wanted to gaff him.

"Your mother likes bluefish," he sighs.

"I know, Dad," I say.

"Partial to 'em myself," he says. "But I won't eat another one till she's home. I won't."

"I know, Dad," I say.

We tread water for a minute or so. It's not uncomfortable or awkward, but it feels . . . incomplete.

"You still scared about going to the high school?" he says, because he apparently prefers awkward and uncomfortable.

"I'm not scared," I say.

He waits a bit, then does this funny lying-down-nodding thing. "Okay," he says. "Neither am I."

When did this become a father-son untruthing competition?

Odd, how waiting can be a job in a conversation, shared or alternated between two people. I outwait his wait. Younger, I have more stamina.

Now that we've got the lying-to-each-other part out of the way, I realize we can do better.

"What if I came with you today?" I say. "I happen to be dog-free for a change."

If his bed were an actual catapult, it would not straighten him up any quicker.

"Really?" he splutters. "Really? Would you like to . . . really, Louis?"

I'm full-blown embarrassed and shocked by how happy this appears to have made him. It feels, in this instant, like the single greatest thing I have ever done. I can't even tell which one of us is the bigger sad sack in this situation, but then again, so freakin' what?

"Yeah," I say. "It'll be Take Your Ne'er-Do-Well Son to Work Day."

"Ah, c'mon, I wouldn't say 'ne'er.' You do well some of the time."

Okay, since he's going to treat this as an actual conversation, we should just move on.

The morning already has a surreal feel to it, even before he queues up his playlist on the car stereo. Sea Shanties. He's bouncing in his seat, humming and singing along with such gusto I can't help laughing.

He stops singing. "What?" he asks me.

"Are you serious with this stuff?" I ask, gesturing at the dashboard.

Keeping his face pointed responsibly roadward, he cuts a quick eye in my direction. "I don't know," he says. "Would that be a bad thing?"

"It would be a hilarious thing," I say. "But not a bad

thing, no. I just had no idea. Sea shanties, Dad?"

He exhales massively, as if he's just executed a great unburdening.

"Right?" he says. "I had no idea myself. It was just something I did, when we first came up here and I moved into fishing. I was a little nervous about the whole thing, and a little lonely. I started half joking, playing the songs to give myself a laugh, but . . . turned out I *loved* the stupid things. Can ya believe that?"

Joy. This is joy, this thing I'm witnessing here right now as my father cranks the volume, bounces in his seat, laughs and sings about sirens and drunken sailors and good men lost to the deep, deep briny.

He hasn't been quite this giddy in ages. I realize how hard he must have been holding on to this secret, and I laugh ten times harder.

The mood is festive, right up to the moment we pull up to the parking space in the boatyard.

"What is he doing here?" I ask as we spy Ike lounging like a lizard over his bike.

"Did I forget to tell you your brother was coming out today?" Dad asks un-innocently. World's worst con man, my father, and it suddenly strikes me as shocking that I ever didn't know about the shanties.

"Yeah, Dad, you *forgot*."

Ike is parked about twenty yards away, by the dock, directly between us and Dad's boat.

"It'll be fun," he says.

"I thought it was gonna be just us," I say, and if I sound like a baby, my only regret is that it's not baby *enough*.

"There were always going to be the fishers," he says. "You knew that."

"They don't count, and you know it," I grunt.

He does know it too. Dad has spoken many times about how alone he feels even on a boat full of people who are paying him to be there.

"You're right," he says somberly. We're both staring out at Ike, who is sunning himself and hasn't noticed our presence. "We were having such fun."

Ma, or her absence, does not enter the conversation.

She floods it.

"Does he have to come?" I say, continuing my crocodilian death roll with maturity.

Dad takes a longer pause than I expected.

"I suppose not," he says, and in that instant, I appreciate how much he, too, is looking forward to our time together.

That answer was so sweet and unexpected, I can't believe I got off that easily. I throw my car door open with renewed vigor.

"I'll leave the decision up to you" is what I sadly hear just before slamming the door.

If this is a test . . . it's a pretty good one. This is not the type of challenge I have ever risen to, and my father knows this as well as anyone. Well played, Dad.

He follows right behind me as we stride toward the boat and the waiting family of customers gathered in front of it.

Ike jumps up off the bike and has a high five waiting above a smarmy smile as I approach him. It's like if the part of the Statue of Liberty will be played today by Ivan the Terrible.

"Woo-hoo!" he says to me, followed immediately by "Oof!" as I jab him in the ribs on my way past.

"Take a hike, Ike," I say, continuing on toward the boat.

Ike squawks out his objections until Dad comes along to calm him right down. Dad has that power in a way nobody else does. And in a few mumbly seconds, Ike is pacified, and the motorcycle is growling off.

Dad is shaking hands with the main man of our fishing party. He seems to be the father of the other three, rambunctious frat types in their late teens or early twenties.

"Back-to-school party," their dad says to my dad. "Thought we'd have a boys' day out together before they all head back to their various colleges."

"Great plan," Dad says, pumping the father's hand, followed by each of the boys'. "It'll be fun and educational all around," he adds, to a big knowing wink from his client.

The guys are enjoying their big day out from the start. As Dad navigates the boat out of the harbor, through a crisp breeze and over a mild chop, the beers are already starting to pop and spritz. They're passing around chicken wings and Doritos and laughing at everything as if it's a filthy joke. They are a truly jolly bunch, and the hilarity is almost infectious, though I don't quite get there. I sip my ginger ale and soothe my ginger stomach. It's always been touch and go with me on the waves, and just witnessing the consumption in front of me is bringing on the gentle jitters.

"All right there, son?" Dad asks, knowing full well. I'm propped on a small bench behind him at the wheel.

"I'll be fine," I say. "Once I get my sea legs under me again. It's been a while."

"Yes, it has. Great to have you aboard, Louis."

"What'd you tell Ike?"

"Told him the truth. That my boy needed some talk time with his dad."

"Is that what the truth is?" I ask.

We hit a solid wave, and Dad spreads his arms wide at it, like *whadja do that for?* He turns back to me. "Well, yeah. Or you could say the dad needs some talk time with his boy. Take your pick. It all comes around the same, don't it?"

"Guess you're right," I say. "So, what is it we wanna talk about?"

Dad laughs, shrugs exaggeratedly. "I dunno. Fish?"

We're out in open water now, and calm. He waves me up to the wheel and points with a slicing hand motion to the horizon ahead. "Just hold steady there, son. I'm going to go and gear these guys up like actual fishermen."

He pounds my shoulder and leaves me to it. In a few seconds I hear whoops and cheers, as if my dad were just back from a very dangerous mission to the Antarctic. There's a lot of jostling back there, and Dad goes into instructor mode. He's very good at it.

I love the open water. The scent of it, the vapor face

it gives you, even the bumpety-bumps that come up from under your feet as you skim over it. The fact that Dad put me at the helm so readily gives me a rush of something I rarely get to feel: the illusion of control.

It also settles my stomach to be in the driver's seat. The focus required to keep things straight, to keep alert to whatever might pop up out of the ocean—and because it's the ocean, *anything* could pop up—keeps you from thinking too much about the quease that still yearns to join the party.

And a party it is. Dad has to give it the occasional, unusual raised voice to make sure these boys are heeding his every word. They are his responsibility while they are on his boat, and anything that is Dad's responsibility is treated with a seriousness bordering on reverence.

Such as his wife, my mother. I know for a fact that Dad brings her along with him wherever he goes. I know it ordinarily, but I know it now far beyond normally. I see her. On that vast horizon. Skipping the surface of the water. Breaching and leaping and submerging again. There, and there, and there. She doesn't look like a mermaid, or a siren, or anything from the stupid movies.

She's a flying fish. I see her, and see her, and see her out there on the glistening sparkling water.

I could do this all day, Ma. And I know you could too. You always loved the water, and it always loved you back.

I am only vaguely aware of the clatter of sounds going on behind me. It feels as if the aquatic everything ahead of me is so much closer than what's going on just at my back. Then it shifts.

WALKIN' THE DOG

"Huh?" I say into the wind as much as my dad's ear. He's swarmed me, like a defensive lineman sacking a quarterback. He's got me from behind, his arms wrapped around my shoulders and chest, his face and my face facing together out toward the flying fish. "Did you say something about a porpoise?" I ask.

He laughs so crisply my ear pops.

"I *said*," he says, "'purpose.' I like what you're doing with the dogs, because it gives you a sense of purpose."

Now we're both laughing, hard and far out toward the flying fish. "So you didn't get me a porpoise, then."

"Maybe for Christmas," he says, nudging me off the wheel. He consults his tracker screen and announces that the bluefish are everywhere out here right now. "We could just drive around for a while and run 'em over. Which is probably about all this bunch will be up to anyway." He gestures back toward our braying, paying customers.

"Are you not being a little hard on them?" I ask. "They seem all right. Like any other amateur fishing party, no?"

"You'll see," he says, cutting the engines way down and coasting to where he figures the prime spot will be. He also takes advantage of the calming conditions to address me again. "It's time, Louis; you know it is. It'll be good for you, and you will be great. You're gonna smash it."

School.

"I know." I huff like I'm starting grade school rather than high school.

"Especially with, y'know, all that's happened. It'll be better for you to be out of the house more. Then, next year, Faye, too. Your mom'll be home soon. I'm gonna start winding all this down." He gestures broadly at the boat beneath us, in a sort of whirlpool motion—which I find a bit unsettling. "It's time for the next phase of life for all of us."

I know. I know every single bit of it is true.

But my father has something like his fish-finder screen that looks into me, as well.

"I can see that you don't completely buy into it yet, Louis, but trust me, you will."

"I trust you, Dad," I say, because it's the absolute truest thing I can say.

He cuts the engines completely, and the boys hoot and holler in celebration.

Possibly premature celebration.

The boat bobs. A lot. I suck on my ginger ale like I'm underwater and this bottle is oxygen.

Ninety seconds later, one boy is hanging over the side. A second one is hanging over the other side. They are honking so hard it's as if they're summoning the deepest of sea creatures to come up to us.

Positioned at the two stations at the rear of the boat, the father and the oldest of the boys laugh hard at the misfortune. I think, maybe, I might laugh along. Dad remains stony. He never finds that sort of muck funny.

Turns out, neither do I. And ginger ale can do nothing about it anymore.

This scene plays out for maybe ten minutes before it feels

like—oh please god—the storm might be blowing over. Dad has taken a seat beside me, rubbing my back. "At least you'll bring up some more fish for us, eh, chum?"

Lest there be any confusion, he is not using the friend version of chum, but the chopped pieces of rotting fish variety.

"Thanks, Dad," I say, just before the commotion starts.

The dad at the back of the boat has a hit on his line, and he is frantically reeling something in. From the assured way he handles it, he is an accomplished fisher and before the fish has had much of a fighting chance, it's up, off the water, in the air, then on the deck.

It's a beautiful bluefish, probably fifteen pounds of angry. It kicks and bucks all over the place, appropriately snapping at everybody who gets too close. Big electric-yellow eyes and millions of sharp, gnashing little teeth. Dad hands the man the pliers, and the guy wrestles the powerful creature under control-ish, until he manages to pull it hard to him and then delicately work the hook out of its mouth.

It's at least as much silver as it is blue, and the sunshine loves it. As it thrashes, it picks up every facet of light as if it were covered in sequins. Its belly is broad and puffy and so blinding white that this great fish certainly must taste like marshmallow.

"Now, men," Dad announces in such a captain's bark of a voice I must quickly look up to remember that it's actually him. Dad leads the other dad, who follows him while commanding his boys to follow.

Just before the steps up to the wheel there is a long, sterile-looking table with drawers underneath. We all gather around my father, who has seized this blue as if it has been his for his whole life.

"This," Dad announces, "is how you do it. And it is the *only* way you do it. Understand?"

The dad calls out that they all do, absolutely, understand. He is staring at his kids as he says it, even though—or because—they only sort of seem to understand.

Oh. I know what this is. I'm aware of it, but up till now have not seen it. A few years ago, around the time she came around to eating bluefish, Ma made some sort of peace with the universe by getting Dad a special gift for his birthday. It was a master class with a famous fish assassin. The man was renowned for being religious about the right method for killing fish, for both ethical decency and deliciousness. He also taught my father to make sushi.

Dad moves quickly and deliberately. He speaks crisply. "Take this," he says, raising something that looks like a giant T-shaped nail and calmly spiking it into a carefully selected spot on the side of its head. "To render it senseless, for obvious reasons." The fish snaps back and forth, naturally, until slowing right back down. Dad then grabs a large, lethal knife and makes a couple of quick incisions in the fish's chest before flipping it around and severing its tail almost completely. "This is to start the bleeding-out process immediately, to slow the decomposition."

Finally he takes a long and sharp metal rod. He sticks it

through the tail cut and all the way up the back under the dorsal fin. "This is to destroy the spinal cord, making certain that your fish cannot feel any residual pain."

The magnificent bluefish goes completely still. And takes all the rest of us with it. Dad gently plunges it into the waiting cooler full of watery ice.

Then he slowly walks back up to the wheel.

I make my way up there to sit with him. Gradually all the fishers retake their spots, and eventually fishing starts happening again.

"Do you always do that?" I ask.

He turns to me with a smile sadder than any frown. "Yup. You wanna fish on my boat, there's a right way, and that way must be learned. Fishing, like life, can be a sumptuous but bloody business. There's no way around that. Nor should there be."

He turns away from me and toward the water ahead. We're not doing anything more than drifting, so there's nothing for him to focus on out there. Except everything, I guess.

The fish start hitting, and the boys start calling. Every one of them, the dad included, winds up needing something or other from my father. He rushes to help land the fish, stun it with a mini club he calls "the Preacher" if the fish is too violent and dangerous, and then does *the thing* that turns the activity from blood sport into a religious service of sorts. Every guy who catches each fish hangs right by Dad's side through the whole process. But in the end, there is only one man seeing each creature across to whatever fishy next world awaits. I half think that if one of those boys really wanted to—which they don't—do the killing, Dad would find an excuse to keep the job to himself.

Not that he appears to enjoy it. It seems to take a little more life out of him each time. Right and wrong, together as one, must be a powerful drain of a force.

Through it all, I sit on the top step, the wheel at my back and the killing table at my feet. Every third fish or so, Dad raises the spike, or the knife, up toward me.

"You want to see one through?" he asks softly, like the killer he is not. He asks it just the same each time.

I shake my head no, the same each time. "Don't think so, Dad," I say.

"Maybe you should, anyway," he says.

"Maybe you're right," I say, shaking my head no.

We're out for nearly four hours total by the time we're back in the inner harbor. None of the guys catch fewer than two fish, and none of the fish are so small they have to be thrown back. The day is a success by any measure—mine as much as anybody's. Dad and I have had a constant stream of salt air and talk that would probably have been unimaginable under any other circumstances. The only breaks in our conversation come when the other dad climbs up to our perch and lets Dad know repeatedly how he cannot tell him how much this afternoon meant to him and his boys.

In between the second and third time he tells him what he cannot tell him, it occurs to me to ask Dad, "Ike . . . he's in line with the whole solemn, ethical killing ritual?"

Dad pauses thoughtfully, but not. "Well," he says, "I do have to hide the Preacher when he's aboard."

It's that kind of day, when things that shouldn't make me laugh are regularly making me laugh. I don't like that Ike's a true brute. I don't like even the humane killing thing, and I know I'm going to have to be filtering it all out of my dreams for a while now.

Fish are not dogs. I know that. It's different.

But I know I saw a dog look at me with those yellow eyes before.

As we're docking, the clients come up to us like a procession. They're offering Dad several gorgeous, gourmet fish. Yes, an offering.

Dad solemnly waves them all away. They don't know why, don't need to know why, but he needs to tell them why. Because he is not a man to insult anybody, anytime, anywhere, and especially not on his very boat.

"When my beloved wifeling is home to share it with me, and not before. But thank you."

The younger guys look puzzled but respectful. The dad, who appears to appreciate oceans, fish, boats and wifelings, bows at the waist and starts packing up the beauteous bounty.

"You properly killed every one of those fish," I say as Dad gently berths the boat. "And it clearly was no fun for you. Nobody in the world would think less of you if you bent your rule and took one home for your dinner."

The boat bumps into the buffers. Then bumps and bumps

again until we are properly parked. Every day he beats out against the current, and then beats again into shore, and I don't even know if he knows the difference under the current circumstances. My father teaches me stuff. As that other dad, through my dad, was teaching his kids stuff.

More than anything, more than he might even realize, he's teaching me how to love somebody. To a scary degree, he's teaching me the power of that.

"I hate even the good and proper killing," he says. "But I'd empty the entire ocean and kill every creature out of it with my own teeth if it would make your mother happy, and make her *here*."

"So," I say, "that's a *no* to bluefish tonight, then?"

It is certainly a testament to some quality or other that my brother possesses—though I cannot figure out what that quality might be—that we find him parked in the same spot where we left him. Dad and I both stop short when we see him. When he notices he's had the desired effect on us, he starts up the bike and revs it mightily.

"I didn't wanna go anyway," he snarls, before zooming madly out of the lot, nearly mowing down our fishing brethren along the way.

"Did he come back just to tell us that?" I ask. Then I shudder. "Or is he mental enough to have sat there stewing all afternoon?"

Dad sighs, shrugs, shakes his head, which about sums up his eldest child, really.

8. Lessons

THE NEXT TIME I GO TO THE BIOMED BEAGLE HOUSE, THE place sounds different. Festive, you might say, and that's not a word that springs to mind about a house that has Willard inside. I'm a bit winded from hurrying because I'm several minutes late.

I'm listening to harmonica music as I stand and press the doorbell. Then I'm listening to harmonica music and Willard barking and the beagles barking back until several seconds later Virginia throws open the door.

"Aaaand *pop* goes the weasel!" Virginia says as a greeting. There's a bit more spirited wheezing on the harmonica, but that's the end of the song. Virginia claps at her own good timing and ushers me inside. Willard sounds almost giddy as he chirps, "It's one of the great songs, because it has both monkeys *and* weasels in it. Genius."

I round into the living room to find Agatha plunked down on the sofa beside Willard. I pause with the shock of it, then start walking toward them. As I do, she starts sort of musically narrating my movements. *Huff-huff*, in-out, *huff-huff*, she makes me sound like a steam train just getting started out of the station. I stop and stare at her. She goes quiet. I start walking toward the dogs on the floor by Willard's feet. She huffs me along again.

"What are you doing here, anyway?" I say, planting myself once more.

"This is the time we set, isn't it?"

"We?" I ask. "*I* remember setting a time, and I suppose you were somewhere in the vicinity when I did. But that doesn't make it a *we* situation, in my opinion."

"In my opinion it does," says Willard. "What's your problem, kid?"

"Yeah, what's your problem, kid?" Agatha says, smiling up sweetly at me.

"What, are you taking Faye lessons?" I say.

"Yeah. It's a trade. I'm teaching her harmonica."

I growl a little, start moving toward where the dog leashes are hanging on a hook by the door to the kitchen. As I walk, I seem to resume making train sounds. I growl some more. Virginia scoots up behind me, whispering, "Aw, is it cookie time?"

"No, ma'am," I say in my stern, busy-businessman voice, "it's not cookie time. It's dog-walking time. But thank you."

"Well, you might find them a little tuckered out. They were walked just a short while ago."

"I walked 'em," Agatha says cheerfully.

I spin forcefully back in Agatha's direction. Virginia intercepts me. "It was just that you were late. And the dogs were so excited to see Aggie."

WALKIN' THE DOG

Agatha silently mouths the word *Aggie* while pointing at herself.

The doorbell rings. Virginia scurries to answer it. She opens it to find her neighbor from across the street, and his companion. Old Man Dan and Amos.

"Hiya," Dan says. "Everything all right? I noticed some strange kid with the bagels, and I was wonderin'..."

"Hiya, Dan," I say over Virginia's shoulder as she not-too-casually bars the door. I think I actually see stink vapor lines wiggling in the air above man and beast.

"Oh, good," Dan says brightly. "I was afraid the arrangement wasn't workin' out."

I'm thinking, *Yes, Dan, you'll get your discount*, but I'm saying, "It's working out great, for everybody. Don't you worry."

"Yes," Virginia says with a small choky hitch in her throat. I notice a sort of heave spasm in her back, too. Fair to say, she doesn't want the Aromatics crossing her tidy threshold. "It's going swell, for everyone. Thank you for the recommendation. In fact, the kids were just heading out the door now to take the dogs for another walk—"

"*Another* walk?" Dan says.

"Yes, *another* walk," Virginia says. "Right, Louis?"

I eventually catch up, but not before Agatha does. She's off the couch and has the leashes, hooking up Buckminster and Magnolia.

"Oh, just Maggie," Willard says. "Too soon for Bucky to go out again."

"Ohhhh," Agatha moans dramatically. "Those adorable wagon wheels..."

"Amos can tag along," Dan says. "Can't Amos tag along?"

"Sure he can," Virginia says. "Well," she whispers to me, "at least I'll only need to launder one of my dogs after this. I'll have a bath ready."

I'm sure at this point she'd agree to give Amos the keys to her car in order to move this along.

Agatha and Magnolia and Amos and myself trip outside and bounce along down the road, as Virginia promises Old Man Dan we will in fact deliver his pungent pal *to his door* shortly. No need to come get him. She shuts her front door with a hyper-neighborly "Toodle-oo" as soon as her words are airborne.

"So, what, are you stealing my clients now?" I say as we march along behind the two dogs. I have Maggie.

"Unholy mackerel, this dog whiffs," she says. She's trailing right in his slipstream, so, good.

"Did you hear me?" I ask.

"Of course I heard you, and of course I'm not stealing your clients. You may like to know, Louis, that some people do things for decent reasons, not just to get paid."

"I do know that," I insist. I know that a lot, in fact, because my own mother is the queen of that kind of do-goodering. Thinking about that, and thinking about her right now, makes me snap at Agatha. "And so, I'm sorry I said that!"

She looks at me with a puzzled expression and snaps back, louder, "Okay, then!" Then she adds, at a more normal volume, "But you should be careful, about being late and stuff. Before you got there, they were talking about how maybe you were taking on too much work to keep up. Come to think of it, I guess I could have stolen your clients if I felt like it. Huh."

I don't like that one bit. Especially the *huh*.

We amble quietly along down the block for a few minutes without a destination. Normally I like to know where I'm going when I'm going. Since this is only really a smokescreen-for-Dan walk, it doesn't really matter, though. Just left and left and left again to drop Amos back home.

We're about to make the first left when I stop abruptly. I reach out and gently take the leash from Agatha. "I'll take it from here," I say. "Should I give you some money? You did do some of the work, after all—"

"I don't want any money," she growls, "not from those nice people, and certainly not from you."

"Oh," I say, feeling myself bend backward away from Agatha's anger.

"Oh," she says, mock-matching my tone perfectly. "That all you can come up with, Louis, 'Oh'? It figures. You know, I only came over here today because I thought it might be fun to hang out with you and those sweet little dogs for a little while. Not *for* anything, just *because*. 'Cause I thought you seemed like a nice kid, and maybe fun to be with. And because you didn't seem like the kind of person who would *ask* another person to hang out. So I thought I'd do it for you. Y'know, help you out there a little bit with your people problem."

My *people problem*. If she is taking Faye lessons, she's getting her money's worth.

We're both still holding on to the handle of Amos's leash. Until Agatha tires of this, and of me, and exaggeratedly shoves it into my hands.

"No," I say anxiously.

"No, what?" she says.

"No, don't go," I say. "We can walk together, if you still want to."

She smiles broadly at me and almost laughs the words "That was really hard for you to say, wasn't it?"

I hate it when people I don't know *know* me.

I'm not too crazy about it when people I do know *know* me, for that matter.

"You're really not trying to steal my business, are you?" I say.

She shakes her head and silently reaches out, to take the leash back, or something. She gently touches my hand first.

Agatha is a toucher. I wish she wasn't. That kind of thing doesn't make me feel good. Or possibly it does, which doesn't make me feel good.

I quickly give her back the leash. I make sure she gets Amos.

I know that Virginia just had us do the second walk because she wanted to politely shoo Old Man Dan away. So this is just sort of a bonus walk, probably more of a bonus than Maggie even wants, and as for Amos, he might not even realize he's being walked at all. So we do a modest little turn around the block and then another, before we head back to return our furry friends to their homes.

"That was a very short trip," Old Man Dan says as I hand him the keys to his dog. "I hope you're not wanting to be paid for this."

I don't answer before heading back across the street to return Magnolia to those nice people and sweet Buckminster with the wagon wheels. Virginia expresses her gratitude with cookies for me and Aggie. Bucky sails past on his adorable wheels, which makes Agatha squeal with pleasure, so it seems like we've spread about as much joy as a couple of dog walkers could for one day.

Then, as we start bopping down the sidewalk away from our good deeds, Aggie touches my forearm. There's that touch again.

"Do you only walk for the purpose of walking dogs?" she asks. "Or do you also do any plain old human walking-around walking?"

I'm looking at her hand on my arm, which is possibly distracting me from deciphering what she's saying, but either way, I'm distracted, and not deciphering very well.

"What?" I ask.

"Would you like to just, like, go walking?" she asks. "I don't really feel like just going home, to be honest. I don't *need* to be home." She says this in a flat, unbouncy, un-Aggie way.

It strikes me that it may be the first thing I've heard her say this way.

"So," she continues, "if you don't *need* to be anywhere,

I thought, maybe, we could go walking? Together? For a while?"

Doesn't seem like a lot, does it? What she's asking? Inside, I go into a full-on panic and come up with probably the worst response possible.

"Okay," I say, "but you know, I charge for this service."

Pause.

Pause.

And pause again.

"Are you calling me a dog?" she asks.

So apparently when you deal with people regularly, it's easy to walk yourself into trouble. She stares grimly at me, and it makes me feel rotten.

"I swear to you, I was not doing that, Agatha."

She bursts out laughing. "I know you weren't," she says.

I'm so relieved at this, I jump right in and do some more blurting. "Would you like to come and meet a big three-legged dog that looks just like a ship's sail?"

She points at me enthusiastically, like I'm really onto something now.

"Yes, I would," she says. "Who wouldn't?"

I have to admit, walking yourself back out of trouble feels *so* good, it almost makes walking into trouble in the first place worth the whole trip.

We head up the route. Along the main street, left down into the valley, and left again up the long slope on the outer edge of the town.

"Have I told you that *my* dog has three legs?" Agatha says

WALKIN' THE DOG

casually, just as we get to the part of the incline where you can hear the effort of breathing through the words.

"No, you never mentioned that," I say. "I didn't even know you had a dog."

"Oh, yeah. I used to have three, and they all lived in my room. Except two of them ran away. They'll be back, though. I know they will. The one that still lives with me sort of has the same name as you, actually."

"You have a three-legged dog who lives with you in your room, and his name is Louis?"

"He spells it differently, though. Unless you spell yours L-E-W-I-S."

My breathing is getting more strained as I speak, and I'm not sure it's the incline that's causing it. "No," I huff. "No, that's not my spelling."

"There ya go," she chirps. "Different name, totally different dog."

Now who's calling somebody a dog? is what I don't say.

The same sweet stuff is happening that always happens on this walk. The air is getting thicker, greener, tastier. The town fades away and the country nuzzles in, and the sense that nonhuman company could be crowding in from all sides becomes intense.

Agatha bumps along beside me, then bumps right into me, with her shoulder.

"I like it here," she says. "It's better than real life. It's nicer."

There are a number of thoughts I think about that. I decide the simple thing is the thing to say.

"You've never been up here, Aggie?"

I look sideways at her as we keep walking, and she shakes her head no.

"How long you been here?" I ask.

We continue walking forward and looking sideward at each other. She shrugs.

I laugh, but it's one of those laughs that don't have to mean you're having a laugh. "You don't know how long you've been living here?" I ask.

She stops looking my way, walks a bit more seriously, straight ahead.

"When a person shrugs, Louis," she says, and there is no shrug about her now, "it can mean a lot of different things. And 'I don't know' is only one of those things. All right?"

She hits that last word with a force that says, it had better well be *all right*.

"All right," I say.

We crest the hill, hit the lushest streak of green archway bending over us, and Agatha gasps.

"I know," I say, "it's cooler than the coolest thing, isn't it? I call it the green tunnel."

She's staring off, away. "It's called a holloway, ya dope," she says.

"What?"

"The green tunnel. It's called a holloway. Anyway, shush. My goodness, she's gorgeous."

I can see now, finally. Up on the edge of the greenness, the *Holloway* bridge between the road and the woods. There's Billie.

She's looking at us. Like maybe expecting us. She's for sure waiting on us, as we approach.

"Gorgeous, Agatha? Are you seeing the same thing that I'm seeing? I mean, she's really something. She's a lot of somethings, but ... gorgeous?"

"Gorgeous," Agatha says, and walks zombielike toward Billie.

It's a funny sensation, but the closer we get—and the more she allows us—the more, possibly, gorgeous Billie gets.

When we finally reach her, she stands, like a queen, like a white marble statue. Agatha extends her hand, upturned, toward Billie's sleek jaw.

When Aggie makes a cooing sound, it seems completely involuntary. She mimics stroking Billie's chin in a sort of *come here to me* motion, and Billie seems to approve. But she stays put.

Even though Agatha and Billie remain with their eyes locked on each other, Aggie for some reason says, "She *knows* you, Louis. She loves you."

Oh, now, please.

See this? Friends. Complicated enough. And girls? And both blended together? I don't get it at all. I don't understand.

"Agatha, she doesn't even look at me. She runs away almost as soon as I show up. And she seems like she's been waiting for *you* her whole life. How do you figure she knows me and loves me and whatever?"

I say all that, and all that makes complete sense. But being real? I want Aggie to come up with an actual, believable answer. I want what she's saying to be true.

"Because she told me," Aggie says flatly.

I'm about to launch into my sensible counterargument. "Oh, come on, how could you even hear what—"

I interrupt myself with an internal head slap, as Agatha raises her hand to cover her gentle laugh.

"You're cute," she says. "Anyway, she told me with her eyes."

It clearly makes no more sense than the talking-dog version, but for some reason I'm prepared to accept it now.

"I hope you're right," I say. "I'd like to take her home."

Agatha starts walking slo-mo toward Billie, and I join her. "Men," she huffs. "Why do you say that? Maybe she *is* home."

"Dogs don't live in the wild," I say. "Certainly not three-legged dogs."

"I don't see why not," Aggie says.

Billie stares at us, even giving a quick, curious head tilt before turning and bolting into the woods again. Her version of *I don't see why not either.*

We'd gotten to spend several minutes with her. "That's a lot more time than she gave me before," I say hopefully.

"Maybe she's breaking you in gradually," Agatha says.

"You think?" I ask.

"Can't be sure. I'll ask her next time."

We continue walking the circuit, taking in the surrounding farms, the hills, and the animals in the dull August haze. We can see everything in the town from the topmost edge of the walk before cresting and heading back in. At one point we can even see the regional high school off in the distance.

"You going there this year?" Agatha asks me, pointing to the school.

"I am," I sigh, like I'm already tired of a place I've never been before.

"That's *so* great," she whoops. "I start in September too. We can go together. We could be, like, school pals. It'll be good to be going in with a friend. Won't it?"

I'm simultaneously overwhelmed with both fear and gratitude over this. I don't really know anybody else going into the freshman class. But at the same time, this feels awfully close to social obligation territory.

I manage to say, "Um . . ."

"Oh no, no," she says, waving her hands in a calming gesture. "Don't worry, Louis, it won't be anything like that. I won't crowd you or embarrass you or anything."

Is my face really that obvious? Maybe she can actually read Billie's thoughts too.

"It'll be great, Agatha," I say, and as I do, I reach out and touch both of her forearms lightly. The kind of gesture she would make, I imagine. How did that happen? "School pals, that'll be cool."

Of the million things we might be, cool isn't among them. But there, I said it. And she looks pleased. It's possible I do too.

9. Momma's Boys

MY PLAN IS TO MAKE AN UNSCHEDULED TRIP OVER TO SEE Ma and tell her all about the pleasant Cyrus surprise. I think she'll be happy to have him for a visit, but as I said, nothing's taken for granted now.

It's a sausage morning. After a whirlwind tour, all eighteen of our legs hammering holy hell out of the pavement, I drop the lovable links back in their garage. Which is wise, because Ma is, of course, a vegetarian. I'm well on my way to the Knoll, striding with purpose and certainty, when a familiar, low, and menacing rumble burbles up from the pavement, through my legs, into my torso.

I used to love the whole Harley-Davidson thing. I found it hypnotic, muscular, and it had just the right kind of outlaw about it. So, weirdly, did Ma, in her hippieish way.

But no longer. No, no, no, no longer. Mr. Davidson now sounds to me like a big, fat blowhard who likes nothing better than the sound of his own relentless farting. I suppose it's not Ike's fault, exactly. Though it's not *not* his fault either. Noise pollution is the pollution that bothers me more than all the others. Because I'm so aware of it, and it's so intrusive, as if it's directed at me. The thing is, it comes *to* me, comes *after* me. Feels personal, is the thing. Sure, I'm probably inhaling fifty million particles of horror with every breath of air I take, but I'm not *aware* of each of those particles as I do, so it's not so bad. Noise irritates me personally. Seriously.

The Harley is just so much louder and more aggressive than it needs to be. And it seems to me more and more that Ike is too. He's the Harley-Davidson of humans, and so frequently irritation sails in on rolls of H-D thunder. There is no irritation like Ike-on-a-bike irritation.

I'm well aware of the motorcycle coming up behind me. Perhaps unconvincingly, I pretend not to notice and continue strolling along. Maybe Ike will buy it, who knows?

As far as brains go, my brother has very big muscles.

"I *said*," he bellows, "wait up!"

I turn to see him curb crawling, and I answer while continuing to walk backward. "Can't hear you," I say, pointing to both my ears in order to help him out as much as I can. I'm good like that.

"I *said* . . . ," he says again.

I heard him the first time, but anyway.

I continue backpedaling, pointing to the Harley now with one hand and making a slashing motion across my throat with the other. "I can't hear you. Maybe if you cut the engine . . ."

I rudely turn my back to him.

He politely cuts the engine. It's rare, and should be acknowledged, that Ike is trying harder than I am.

I continue walking away.

"If you keep going ...," he says.

It doesn't sound like much, but we both know. As of those words, the number of directions this could take is a very small, painful number.

I stop, turn, and stroll casually back to where he's sitting.

"Where you been?" he asks me.

"Just walkin' the dogs," I say.

"That's what you always say lately."

"Maybe that's because I'm always walkin' the dogs lately."

"Unless you're out walkin' the *fish*," he says triumphantly.

That counts as a very clever gotcha in Ikeworld. Fortunately, my will to live is stronger than my will to laugh. Just barely, though.

"That's what this is about," I say. "You're here because we didn't take you out fishing with us."

"*We?*" he snarls. "What are you, a *we* now?"

Really, if he doesn't knock off the comedy, my will to live might not win the day. "Ah, my father and me? Yes, I'd say we qualify as a we."

"Not without me, ya don't." Ike wins more fights than he loses, but not without taking a lot of shots to the head. "Anyway, you guys don't need to *take* me anywhere. Who the hell do you think you are?"

All jokes aside—and I am struggling to set them aside—he seems genuinely upset about this. That should make me happier than it does.

"I'm sorry, Ike. We . . . Dad and I . . . needed that time

together. It was nothing personal." One of those statements was true at least.

We stand in silence as he works out the correct response. What he comes up with is "Don't let it happen again."

"Okay," I say. "I won't . . ." . . . *let you know if it ever happens again.*

"Who's that kid you were with the other day?" he demands, shrugging off his moment of humanesque vulnerability like a boxer shedding his robe.

I have no idea how he knows who I was with, because if he was tailing me, I would have heard the bike a mile off. Don't know how he knows, but I know he knows. He always knows.

I start to answer. "Funny, that was—"

"I know who he was," Ike says. "Don't you wonder why he lives in Chernobyl? The only people who live in there—"

". . . Are Chernobleens?" I ask. "Chernobobs?"

He stares at me blankly. "You know I know everything you do, Louis, right? You know I know every move you make, every think you think. I know everything. I know more about you than you do."

"You do?"

"I do."

"Then why do you need to ask me if I know that you know? You must already know the answer."

He stares at me for many seconds, which I love. Because I rarely get the upper hand in these things. Every confused blink of his heavy-lidded eyes—and there are many blinks within a short span of time—feels like a drummer smashing a cymbal. *Bash! Bash-bash-bash.* This can't last.

"I never liked that kid," he says. "The whole time Ma was tutoring him, I wanted to wipe that smile off his face every time I came in the house."

"I don't recall him ever smiling when you came in the house."

"Good," he says. "That's good."

"Wiped the smile right off Ma's face at the same time. Remember that, Ike? She couldn't stand the way you treated Cy. Same way she couldn't stand most of the things you did. Why was it again you didn't like Cy? I never quite worked that out."

He is unruffled, sitting there on his mechanical throne, sure of himself and his perch on the world.

He shrugs. "I don't need a reason. Do I need a reason, Louis? Maybe I'm just one of those people who know people intuitively. Maybe I just knew he was a smug so-and-so right outta the chute. Like he was superior or something."

"Cool. Wow. Y'know, Ike, I got a theory—"

"Don't want to hear your theory, Louis. I never want to hear those."

Even better. "My theory is that maybe, Ma wouldn't be where she is now if you made a little more effort. You're, like, the anti-Ma, the way you're always making the world a more angry and horrible place. Did it ever occur to you that that hurts her? News flash, Ike: she's a very sensitive person."

The reason I can get away with this stuff is, Ike doesn't care. At all.

"You say 'sensitive' like it's such a great thing," he says with a laugh. "You know, little man, I've been thinking about you a lot lately."

"Oh, please, Ike, don't do that."

"Too late. And I've been thinking you're a lot like Ma. *Too* sensitive. And with the way things are going—"

"Shut up."

"The way things are going, with high school coming at ya, with the situation with Ma going who-knows-where—"

"*I* know where. She's gonna be fine, *that's* where."

"That's not a place. Anyway, the thing is, you're not ready, kid, not ready for *shit*. The world's a big bowl of suck, and you're not prepared for it. You aren't tough enough to face reality, and for this, I blame myself."

"Please, Ike, whatever you do, don't blame yourself. It's making the hair on my neck stand up just hearing that."

"Good. That's a start. So somebody's gotta make a man outta you, and it sure won't be Dad. And face it, Ma's not gonna be around to baby you forever—"

I'm no doubt just adding fuel to his noxious fire, but I slap my hands over my ears, spin, and start marching down the road.

"Get on the bike," he barks.

"Oh, no, thanks anyway," I say, pointing down the street. "I'm just gonna walk. Gonna visit Ma. Nice day and everything. I'll tell her you said hi."

He waits the requisite, intimidating amount of time.

"Louis," he says, low. "I'll take you there. We'll visit her together. We'll show her that we're making nice. We'll be a *we*."

Ike and I have not seen each other in a couple of weeks. I have no idea how long it's been since he's seen Ma. I hope it's a long time. He makes her very tense and upset. She wouldn't tell him that, though.

"That'll be nice," I say, because words don't have to mean anything if you don't want them to.

I swing my leg over as he powers up the diabolical machine, and the world trembles with it.

My mother and my brother could hardly be more different people. And yet she seems to have some sort of affection for him anyway. It's a parental thing I hope to never have to understand.

"Well, this is a pleasant surprise," Ma says as we stroll in together.

"You mean me, right?" we both say at the same time.

"I mean the two of you, together. You are both pleasant. And both surprising. Brotherly love breaking out all over, that's what I want to see."

This time we do not speak with one voice.

"Sure thing, Ma," Ike says. "Best buddies." He even gives me an exaggerated, hard squeeze with his big paw draped over my shoulders.

I hate it when I have to choose between my mother's happiness and the truth. But the truth never made me sticky rice with tomato sauce and ricotta with tiny veggie meatballs.

"Best buddies, Ma," I say.

She knows. "You're a sweet little liar," she says to me with a deliberately cheesy, no-less-brilliant smile. Then, as quickly as it came and like pulling the sheet down to unveil a statue, the smile slides away to the floor. These quick-shiftings are not new. I still can't get used to them.

Even Ike can see it. And he's a dolt.

"Ma," he says, "not to worry. We're fine. We really are. Right, Louis?"

"We are, Ma, honestly," I say, somewhat short of honestly.

"The kid just needs the occasional lesson, about the real world. And that's what I'm here for, to teach him valuable real-world lessons."

I can hear myself gulp the way cartoon characters express nervousness.

"Well," Ma says, "I have to admit, I know there are a great many real-world lessons my younger son needs to learn. But I hope my older son helps him *gently* through those lessons."

Go, Ma.

"Am I ever not gentle?" Ike says, sounding wounded. He punctuates it with a bit of a chuckle.

Ma appears to have lost the thread of the discussion. Or possibly just the will to follow it. She backs up, without looking, and settles onto her bed when she bumps into it.

"Are you okay?" Ike asks her.

"Look around," I say to him. "Of course she's not okay."

"You look like you could use some fresh air, Ma," he says. He's right about that. Her skin looks like it's coated in a light skimming of yesterday's oatmeal.

"I know," she says. "I haven't been outside in some time."

"You haven't?" he says aggressively. When there is something to aggress against, Ike will always be your man. He can make even an apparently concerned gesture cause you to feel like you need to put on a helmet.

"The staff don't like for me to go out without somebody available to keep an eye on me."

"I'll keep an eye on you," Ike says, marching toward the nurses' station.

"I don't think they mean you," she says. "Somebody official-like."

"Official-like? Do they know I am an officer of the law?"

I figure he's out of earshot when I work up the courage to say, "Everybody, everywhere, knows you're an officer of the law."

He was possibly not quite out of earshot. "Somebody needin' another respect lesson so soon?" he calls back.

As is normally the way with such things, the situation is sufficiently bent to Ike's will that within five minutes the three of us are strolling around the grounds. The Knoll is sitting under a partly sunny, wholly pleasant sky. The place is built on a hill and situated in such a way that you can see manicured lawn and bushy flowering hedges in every direction. There are reasonably busy roads all around, but while you can hear them, they don't intrude on the sights unless you head down the long rose-lined driveway for a hundred or so yards.

It seems Ma did indeed need this air, as within minutes she looks altogether revived. We follow a sort of corkscrew pathway down, circling the main hill of the grounds until we reach a serene little resting spot with some benches placed around a central stone fountain and a statue of a saintly looking nun.

Despite the presence of my brother, this is the nicest visit I've had yet to this place. Unlike when she's in her room, or the dining area, Ma looks truly happy and comfortable right here. Even Ike gives off an air of something like humanity.

But I hate it.

"When are you coming home again, Ma?" I ask.

She responds with one of the touchstones of my childhood.

"We'll see," she says, with a reassuring little giggle to soften words that don't reassure me one bit. She used to whip that one out to counter everything she wouldn't, or couldn't, properly answer. It frustrated me to the point of tears almost every time. I feel the same way about it now.

"Leave her alone, Louis," Ike says. "She'll come home when she's ready. You just need to be a big boy for her now, and suck it up, buttercup."

Because pressure brings out the creative in me, I say, "*You* suck it up."

"Please," Ma says, "both of you suck it up."

Ike laughs out loud, because it's quite funny to hear that come out of Ma. Then she laughs at Ike's laughter. Then, okay, all right, I have to laugh along with them.

Who'd have thought? A round-robin of hilarity I never would have predicted.

Then, gone again.

"I should be getting back," Ma says nervously.

"But we just got here," Ike says.

"No, it's time," she says, and starts corkscrewing back up the mini mountain toward the safety of her tower once more.

She loves being outside, though. This is a fact. Ike and I look at each other, shrug, and light out after her. She's fast when she wants to be.

We never catch up to her. By the time her two strapping lads make their way back to the Knoll and up to her room, Ma is rather relaxed, on her bed, feet up, with the baseball game on the TV. She's only recently become a sports fan. Good for her, she missed the previous nine decades or so of Sox-stress. She only knows the good stuff.

"Listen, we're gonna go," Ike says, when it becomes apparent that our departure will mean a lot less than whether the Sox's pitching coach is signaling to bring in a righty or lefty from the bullpen. It's only the fifth inning, for crying out loud. The bullpen should still be sleeping.

"Oh," she says, not exactly faking interest in us as she reaches out for hugs, but not exactly not.

"Okay, Ma," Ike says, giving her a firm and rapid hug before pivoting enthusiastically for the exit.

"Okay, Ma," I say, giving her my version of firm but lingering longer. "Y'know, I ran into Cyrus. You know Cy. Remember when you tutored Cy . . . ?"

She lets out an exaggerated *sigh*, like I used to do.

"Yes," I say. "That's it. That's him. Cy. Great kid. You taught him. He loved you. And everybody loved *him*."

"Right," she says brightly, as if the Sox's pitching coach has selected exactly the right reliever. "Everybody *loved* him."

"That's right. Everybody loved him, right, Ike?"

Ike has made it to the hall and can't be too pleased to have to poke his blocky head back into the room. "We have to get going," he hisses.

"Love," I say. "We were talking about love. How lovable Cy always was. And how much you and I love our mother and love to make her happy, yeah? Love."

"Right," he says. "Love."

That word has never sounded greasier. I feel some sense of accomplishment there, and it maybe goes to my head a little.

"And like, what's not to love, right?" I say. "The guy's smart, good-looking, polite, considerate, doesn't ride a disgusting loud motorcycle or ever upset his mother or anybody else's—"

Not only does Ike's yank pull my shoulder out of its socket, but it nearly pulls the opposite shoulder through my torso along with it.

Ma continues watching the game as she waves us off.

Once he's dragged me down the stairs and out the door, beyond where any trained medical folk can help me, my brother starts on me. He's grabbed me by the back of my shirt and is bouncing me like a marionette along the path toward his motorcycle.

"Think you're pretty cute, do ya?" he says.

"That's not for me to say," I say.

He jerks me remarkably high into the air, then brings me back down with a *whomp*, face-first into the grass. He lands heavily on top of me, and today's lunch will be a big mouthful of turf.

I spit the words and dirt out together. "Jealousy isn't a good look on you."

Whomp.

"Good point," I add. "Nothing's a good look on you."

I should know better. I do, really, except that I obviously don't.

Ike shifts forward and, from the feel of it, leans on the back of my head with both forearms. He speaks to me in a relaxed fashion. He could have his elbows on a little circular table for two in a classy coffeehouse as he imparts his wisdom. Except that Dunkin' Donuts doesn't have small circular tables for two, and as far as he is concerned, every other coffeehouse in the land can just go someplace wicked and do terrible things to itself. Or words to that effect.

"Y'know, Louis," he says, "that punky kid is bad news."

"Huh," I say pensively, a pensive *huh* being the only sound I can currently make.

"I don't like your choice of friends."

To be honest, I don't really have many. And choice doesn't come into it as much as happenstance does.

"Huh," I say pensively.

"I fear I have been neglecting your real-world education, little man. And now is probably a good time to start remedying that situation. For starters, you keep that boy well away. Got it?"

I say, "Not got it," but it sounds remarkably like a pensive *huh*.

10. Cordially Invited

"We have mail," Dad says, coming through the front door and leafing through letters as he normally does. I never bother with any of it, from the time it all tumbles through the slot till the time Dad comes in several hours later to scoop it up. Because it's never for me. None of it. Never.

Until now.

I'm sitting at the table by myself, having my solitary dinner. Things have drifted this way a lot lately, away from our nuclear-family meals and more toward lackadaisical individuality. I'm having the soup-and-sandwich option, minestrone from a can and a chicken club. It's a sad little club where chicken isn't even a member and the members include bologna plus one straggler slice of salami, crappy useless iceberg lettuce that actually lets out a sigh when I bite into it, and yellow mustard on a white burger roll. I don't know how these ingredients even got into the house, but it never would have happened on Ma's watch. It's a meal of surrender.

"How do 'we' have mail?" I ask.

He slides into the seat next to me and slaps my letter down on the table. Then he waves an identical-looking one addressed to him.

They're both from the School. Not this beloved school right here, in which I live. But the big bad wolfy place I will be attending in a very short time.

"You wanna go first?" he asks

I shake my envelope around excitedly, like a lottery winner. "Oh, let's do it together," I squeal. Maybe it's not quite a squeal, but it feels like a squeal.

"You know, Louis," he says, blinking exaggeratedly at me, "sarcasm is the lowest form of humor."

"Yeah?" I smarm, "bet I can go lower." It must be the lettuce talking.

He snags the letter right out of my hand and quickly tears both of them open. "It's a party invitation," he says brightly.

"It is no such thing," I say, snagging right back.

I didn't notice Faye come into the room. From behind me, she grabs the letter out of my hand and starts reading.

"'We are pleased to invite all the members of our incoming freshman class, along with their parents or guardians, to join us for our annual greeting and orientation day, where you will get to know your new educational home, the facilities, the staff, and above all, your cohort of...'"

Snag. The letter is back in my possession. It states that the date in question is only eight sleeps from now. That's not nearly enough sleeps. Dad is still reading to himself, and Faye is laughing, as I calmly say, "Nah..."

"You can't say nah," Faye says to me. "He can't say nah to something like this, can he, Dad?"

Dad silently finishes his reading, looks up, and says, "This is not a house where we tell people they can't say nah—"

"Nah it is, then," I chirp.

"Maybe they should offer Louis an orientation-into-normal-human-life day first, before they attempt the freshman thing."

"Faye," Dad says. "Stop being helpful."

"Okay," she adds, "but I really could be helpful if you want. I could come along as the big baby's emotional support animal."

"Jeez," I say, "when you put it like that . . . *nah!*"

"Son?" Dad says, in a sweet and beseeching way that makes me furious every time he does it.

"Daaad?" I drawl, in the standard response way that is the verbal equivalent of a cat resisting a bath.

"It'll be a good thing," he says reasonably. He politely waits out my nonresponse before adding, "Would you really make me go to this by myself?"

"Ha!" Faye yelps, and then claps repeatedly like one of those windup monkeys with the cymbals.

"Grr," I say.

"Please, just give it some thought?" he says.

We all know I'll need some alone time for this. I'm about to clean up after myself when Dad says, "No, Faye will take care of that. Faye? Will I make us some dinner?"

"No, allow me," she says, moving about the kitchen all

domestic-like while Dad sits happily at the table and starts chatting chummily with her.

Oh, great, I think as I slink toward my room, *they're gonna* discuss *me now.*

But once I've hopped up onto my bed, I throw everybody a curveball—including myself—by texting Agatha.

I don't get too ambitious, for starters.

Hello, Agatha.

When I say her response takes seconds, I mean, like four of them.

What. Are you OK? Hostage situation? Trouble down at the old mill? Blink three times if you're not free to speak.

She succeeds in making me mad and making me laugh. She can only be allowed to know about one of those.

Listen you. I am as good at texting as the next person.

As long as the next person has no thumbs?

I can't believe I started this. All by myself, with no external pressure from anyone. This thought apparently takes more time rolling around my head than it should.

That would be the equivalent of heavy breathing. What you're doing there. If we were on the phone

As poorly as this is going, I'm *so* glad we're not on the phone.

So am I

This freaks me out enough to force me to jump up off the bed.

How did you do that, Aggie?

I wait anxiously for her response.

And I wait. I pace. And I pace.

I was heavy breathing. See what I did there? Did it feel just like in a horror movie?

Yes it did. Did you get that school letter about orientation day?

There's a pause that doesn't sound like heavy breathing. I'm learning things quickly.

Agatha?

Yes I got it.

Well are you going?

No.

I wait for more. With Aggie there's never not more. Maybe that's just live-action Aggie more than text Aggie.

Why not?

Parents say they can't go. Work stuff.

Oh. Too bad. Your kinda thing I would think.

And you would think correctly. You going?

For some stupid reason, I failed to anticipate this turn in the discussion. I am stutteringly unprepared to answer.

She is not at her most patient. Whatever that would be.

My phone rings. I tentatively answer. I hear her on the other end, huffing and wheezing as if she's the murderer calling from my own basement.

"Why wouldn't you answer me?" she asks in an underpowered—for her—tone.

"I was working on it," I say.

"It wasn't the kind of question where counting on your fingers and toes would help."

"Ha, joke's on you, 'cause it did. I'm not going either, so there."

Somewhere in my data bank of Aggie experiences, I sensed a few possible reactions here. But sadness wasn't in the mix.

"You *need* it, though." She sighs. "Really, Louis, orientation will be the best thing for you. Go."

"You sound like my dad. He's threatening to go without me if I bail. Maybe I should loan you my father and you can go together like a complete set."

"Yes!" she yelps. "Yes, yes, yes, what a brilliant idea, Louis."

What was I thinking? What was I expecting? Of course she took the offer seriously. And of course it would probably make sense. But, no.

"Fine," I say, playing myself like a chess grand master and knowing what happens four moves down the line, "we'll go together. The three of us," I say before she can.

"Woo-hoo," she shouts, tingling my eardrum.

"Calm down," I say, so calmly I almost believe myself. "This is not that big a deal, Aggie."

"Pffft," she says. "I bet this is what you wanted all along."

"It isn't—"

"That's why you called me in the first place, ya sly dog."

I'm not a sly dog. This is not what I wanted. Is it?

Is it?

"I didn't even—"

"Gotta go," she says. And does.

11. Not So Good Samaritan

AMOS REMAINS MY FAVORITE DOG. YOU KNOW HOW I know Amos is a great dog, despite the smell, and the way he does little vomits with the same frequency and volume as a pro baseball player spits tobacco juice, and the way we have to stop fifty times per walk for him to chew on irrational things like fire hydrants and loose hunks of asphalt?

Faye actually asks to come along when I walk him now. That's how I know.

And she complains—in high comedy terms—the whole way. Even though nobody's forcing her.

"You know that thing Dad does?" she says just before we collect Amos this fine morning. "Y'know, where you go into the bathroom after he's had his coffee and his muffin. And the wallpaper's, like, rolling right down off the walls? Well, here we are, walking along in the open, fresh air, and hairy Anus here is peeling the wallpaper off the whole poor neighborhood."

"Nobody asked you to do this," I say. "You can go home anytime."

She opts not to, because of her affection for Amos. We collect him and take him on the riverside walk that he enjoys so much. It's usually not as packed as the dedicated dog parks, where I can tell Amos is shunned by many of the more precious doggy families because of his ... earthy qualities. There's one guy with an Afghan hound who departs the park immediately as soon as we show up. I have to admit there've been a couple of times I went there just hoping to make that happen. I'm not proud of that. Okay, I am.

"Remember when you had that great idea about getting Agatha to work with you?" Faye asks me.

"Um, I remember when I specifically did *not* have that idea," I say. "But please, do go on."

"I was thinking that you maybe should go ahead and hire her."

"What's the matter, business not so good on your end?" I ask.

"Turns out, making the flyers was my favorite part of the job. I don't wanna do what you do, Louis. Never did, to be honest. But it appears that Aggie is all gung-ho about it. And she's driving me a little crazy now. You're getting busier all the time, so . . ."

"Ah," I say, clapping and rubbing my hands together greedily like an old-fashioned movie bad guy. It's not often I get to press a moment of advantage over Faye.

She takes note. "Really, Louis? You think this is the wise way to play this?"

I stop rubbing the hands and let them slide slo-mo down

beside me. It's embarrassing how easy this is for her, but it would surely be worse if I escalated.

"I'll think about it," I say.

Faye and I sit on the riverbank as we let Amos do his thing. His thing amounts to dashing in and out of the water and snuffling around all over for remnants of picnics, which unfortunately, the local slobs are too happy to leave behind.

We're sitting for two minutes when Amos comes bounding up to me with a nearly fully loaded corncob in his chops. Corncobs are absolute perfection in Amosworld.

After trying and failing to convince him to let me have the cob, we finally wind up in a wrestling match over it. You might guess at least one of us is having a fun time here, and you would be right.

However, that one would be Faye.

"Why don't you just let him have it?" she asks through a low, rumbling giggle.

"Why?" I ask, as if this should be the most obvious thing in the world. "Because I'm the one who has to see the whole nasty thing *twice*, on the way in and on the way out. And let me tell you . . ." I retch a little in the attempted relaying. "Just, *no*."

I win the battle of the cob, then deposit it in the trash bin over Amos's snuffly objections. He's gotten over it within seconds, as one of his favorite pals appears, a water spaniel known for excellent reasons as the Craptain. The two of them blast off, running up and down alongside the river as well as in and out of it. They pour themselves into a full course of zoomies and bities until Amos comes rushing over, collapsing in the grass between Faye and me. We see the Craptain zoom off again upstream, disappearing just as quickly as he appeared.

"Who *was* that masked man?" Faye asks.

"He prefers to remain anonymous," I say. "I've never even seen his owner."

Just as quickly, I lose Faye. I shouldn't be surprised that she has actual friends—people do that, I hear—but when a pal of hers walks by and Faye drops me just like that, it still feels like abandonment, and I believe I know how Amos feels right now.

He comes up and fills the Faye-shaped space beside me in the grass. More than fills it, actually, but under the circumstances I should be neither selective regarding my companions, nor unkind.

Truth is, I'm happy to have him. Even at this close range.

I brought a string cheese for just such an eventuality.

It's such a huge pleasure, giving a piece of cheese to a dog. You don't have to tell yourself that he loves you for it. In fact, you really shouldn't. It's cool that he loves the *cheese*. And you gave it to him. And that's enough. That's way more than enough.

Dogs have a lot of socially questionable habits. But they don't litter—except in the one big obvious way that isn't their fault—and they don't spit.

To litter, like to murder, you must be conscious of the offense. Only people can do that. It's what separates us from the beasts.

And it seems that beasts sure do love hanging out by the river. There is litter all over. In some places the greatest concentration of trash is located in the immediate vicinity of a half-empty trash can. Like it's all some big joke and the litter receptacle is the punch line.

Even Amos is disgusted, and he is famously no neat freak. I'm shaking my head, appalled at it all, as I turn in the direction of casa Amos.

Almost immediately we run into Faye again. She doesn't have her friend with her, but she does have *a* friend.

Agatha is down on all fours, picking up rubbish. I lay a quizzical look on my sister. She shrugs me equal puzzlement.

"Aggie?" I say.

She jumps to her feet, her mitts full of chip bags and candy wrappers, her eyes glassy, brimming wet.

"Didn't you see any of this?" she pleads.

"Well, I did," I say, trailing behind Aggie on the way to the bin. Faye and I exchange helpless looks.

"And you just did nothing?"

"Not nothing, Aggie. I was appalled. Just before I ran into you, I was thinking about how appalled I was. And I pretty rarely get appalled."

She dumps the trash violently into the bin, then turns on me. "Well," she snaps, "I guess that's okay, then. Louis is appalled, so the world will just be all better now."

Because I am who I am, I take this all in and realize I'm the worst person on earth and the source of all the universe's ills. For a second that makes me feel powerful, which is probably not the right way to go with this.

Because Faye is definitely not me, she says, "Do you think

maybe you're being a little bit harsh there, Aggie?"

Aggie stands, feet wide apart, and breathes many times in a few seconds. "A little," she says.

We all stand staring for a minute, until Faye breaks the quiet tension. "You have to understand, Agatha. Louis doesn't actually *do* stuff."

That would be the end of Faye defending me then. "Oh, I get it," Aggie says. "You're more the bystander type. Am I right?"

"Grr," I say, looking down at Amos and wishing he was grr-ing on my behalf. Why won't anybody grr for me?

"Hiya, stinky boy," Agatha says, bending down to pet the dog and hovering dangerously close to his exhale holes.

I seize my moment.

"I'm sorry," I say rapidly so that it hurts less.

"What are you sorry for, Louis?"

"For, I guess, *bystandering.*"

She remains, heroically, down in Amos's face. "Yeah," she says, "you really do stink. You're awful. Rancid, one might say—"

"All right, all right, I get your point," I say.

"Okay, then you can walk me home, I guess," she says.

Of the stinky boys, Amos is the one who catches on more quickly. He's doing his imbalanced stumble-dance of excitement. He's doing circles on the sidewalk and madly wagging— which I call *fanning*—his tail all around as we start walking along together. It's less than a ten-minute walk to the house, and she clearly didn't need me or anybody else to assist her in getting there, but Amos and I are both happy to have tagged along. Faye does her shrug of agreement, or at least of nonresistance.

There's a long tree-bunchy driveway to where Agatha indicates she lives. It takes almost as long to get down it as it took to get here to begin with. Finally we emerge onto the place itself, and I have to make some effort not to be slack-jawed about it.

The house is what my mother would refer to as a McMansion while making that face like when you accidentally bite into the sour pickle you demanded they leave out of your veggie burger.

"That's where you live?" I ask.

"Yup," she says.

"Then why are you talking to *me*?" I ask.

She sighs dramatically and hands back the leash I surrendered to her for the whole of the walk. "Because you say fun, stupid stuff like that, and I don't think I know anybody else who does. It's funny."

"Fun-stupid," Faye says. "Bullseye."

"You like that, Aggie?" I say. "Then stick around. I'm a total riot once I get going."

"Riot," Faye echoes.

"I'll count on that," she says, walking backward toward her cream-colored castle with all the balconies.

As I'm walking away, I'm scolding myself, thinking, *Why'd I have to go bragging like that? I'll never live up to it.*

She's almost in the door, we're almost to the bend in the driveway—the driveway has a *bend*—when I realize I can't be counting on good luck to keep running her into my path. Faye seizes Amos and I plant myself, calling out.

"We should do this again." I must have heard it in a movie.

What am I doing? I don't know. I've never done it before. Or anything else like it. Then I figure out a way to make it worse. "You should come work with me," I blurt. "I could really use your help."

Agatha comes walking back our way. And, dogs being the caring and intuitive best friends they are, Amos creates a bit of diversion for me. Faye, about twenty feet farther along, sighs with disgust.

It's colossal. And rank. And in the middle of the driveway. *How* did he manage to get that corncob again?

Agatha gets a little dramatic, but probably no more than the situation requires. She points at it.

"I'm surprised he didn't need a midwife to help him deliver that," she says.

"It's a glamorous life," I say.

"It is," she says. "But I'm afraid I still can't help you with it. I'm loyal, y'see. And Faye needs me."

I hear my sister half cough behind me and then start to say something. But for once I beat her to the verbal punch.

"I understand, Aggie. And I respect that. You should stick with Faye."

"That I will," she says sweetly. She waves cheerily.

"How did you find her today anyway?" I say to Faye as we trek down the driveway and back to town.

She's drifted behind me. Pauses before answering so that

she can punch me hard in the kidney for the crime of *not* hiring away her lone employee. "She was just, suddenly, *there*," she says. "She's everywhere. It's like she never goes home."

"She told me she doesn't like to be home," I say.

"If that was my home, I'd never leave it," Faye says. "I'd be there *all the time*."

"Did you know she was rich?" I ask.

"Nope. She doesn't seem like rich. Doesn't *smell* like rich."

"Ha." I snort. "What does rich smell like?"

"Smells the same as Amos, pretty much."

"Now you sound like Ma," I say.

"Good. *Somebody* has to."

12. Why Not?

I'M MORE THAN A LITTLE SURPRISED TO FIND CY AND Pierre sitting on the curb outside my house.

"What're you doing here?" I ask. It doesn't come out the way I intended. "Good to see you, though."

"Yeah, well, we said we'd go and visit your mother, remember?" he says, sounding as sure as if we had agreed on this very minute. I'd pay a lot for that kind of certainty. About anything.

"Um, yeah," I say, catching a quick peek at the time on my phone. We're still within visiting hours. "You mean, now?"

"Yeah. And isn't it about time you told me where she is? I already worked out that she's not here, but . . ."

I sigh loudly at Cy.

"Why not?" he says, somehow managing what I'd call a shrug of certainty. I'm reminded again how I think that is the exact way dogs make every single choice in their lives. Chase something, chew something, eat something, bark at something, pee on something, get overly friendly with something or get overly unfriendly with something? Dogs run it all through the same rigorous testing process. Why not? If they don't come up with a compelling answer to that question, that means go for it.

Why not? Indeed, why not?

"Sure," I say, shrugging with far less conviction.

On the walk, I explain how Ma is not in a hospital, and how she is most definitely coming home soon, and all the other stuff I need to hear myself tell him. Once that's out of the way and Cy doesn't press me with uncomfortable follow-up questions, I push things a little bit further. I tell Cy about the incident at the riverside. I don't know why I do it, and I can't imagine myself telling that to anybody else.

"And you just walked through all the garbage?" he asks, sounding mystified.

"What would you have done?" I ask.

"Not sure. Something, though. Picked up some of the trash, maybe?"

"All right," I say. "I didn't mean to ask for *specific* options."

We walk along quietly for a while, until he speaks up again. "Just, nothing? At all? Couldn't pick up a single can or something?"

I display my well-developed nothingness skills by going completely silent, staring at the ground as we walk.

Eventually, we reach the Knoll. I convince Cy that it would be good to remove Pierre's executioner mask before bringing him inside, because why burden him with a reputation he doesn't need right out of the chute? He says it'll be fine, because Pierre bit an older person once and didn't like the taste.

Funny, we don't talk about Ma much at all before we're all the way into the lobby, standing waiting for the elevator. Finally he asks.

He's looking the place all up and down as the elevator pings our floor. "What's a nice gal like your ma doin' in a joint like this?" he asks as we step aboard.

I remember that was one of the things Ma liked about Cy, his habit of talking like an old-time movie character. I also remember that I liked it myself and tried to copy it.

"Gettin' better, that's what she's doin'," I say. "Same as everybody else."

"I *mean*," he says as we approach our destination, "what's she in for?"

I'm really warming up to this game. And to avoiding his question.

"Thirty days," I say, smiling and leading him out into the hallway.

"Well played, sir," he says, following along and pressing the subject no further.

Less than a minute later, we're standing, all three of us, all eight legs, in Ma's doorway. She's sleeping. Possibly I should have called ahead. She does a superhuman amount of sleeping lately. We enter quietly, Pierre sniffing low and Cy sniffing high, to check out the place while we await my mother's consciousness.

"Fatigue," I say.

"Huh?" Cy asks.

"What she's here for," I say. "Fatigue."

"Okay," Cy says.

"If I were a celebrity, they'd call it 'exhaustion,'" Ma pipes up.

"Um, she's awake," I say.

"Um, even Pierre knows that," Cy says, gesturing at the eighty pounds of dog draped half across my mother in her bed. "Anyway, you *are* a celebrity, Ms. Singletary."

Ma looks intently at Cy. She tilts her head inquisitively. She ruffles Pierre's thickly furred face.

"Do I know . . . ?" she asks, then it clicks. "Wait, I know this fella. Sure I do."

"You're the only person I know who uses the word 'fella,' Ms. Singletary," Cy says, beaming at her.

Frankly, she's the only person I know who uses it too.

The fog is lifting from Ma. The fog we see too often these days.

"How'd you do on those SATs, young fella?" Ma asks, not quite yet remembering who Cy is, but almost.

"I killed them," Cy says, at the same time Pierre completes his vault up into the bed with Ma. She hugs him hard, and he lets her. "That's what I came here to tell you."

Ma pulls Pierre closer to her, in a mighty squeeze. She has him firmly by the neck, his giant head pressed against her small one. I worry she might smother in the bigness of his face. Her eyes go way wet, and she regards Cy hard with those wet eyes.

"We did well, you and I," she says to Cy. "We did good work together."

Pierre might be in some jeopardy, due to the force of my mother's loving, deathly grip on him.

"We did very well," Cy says.

There is a long pause, during which Ma holds on to Pierre. He likewise shows no inclination to break away. But it's a long time. And it feels funny.

"I'm sure you boys have someplace to be," Ma says, letting go of Pierre and pushing him away.

"Actually, Ma," I say, "not really just now—"

"I'm sure you do," she says, both firmly and weakly.

"Well, no place *better*, Ms. Singletary, and that's the truth."

She is charmed by him, as ever. She perks up, and we settle in for quiet conversation and Pierre-stroking.

Most of the talk, honestly, is between Ma and Cy, and I am happy with this. As they chat, about academic stuff and good citizen stuff and how proud Cy's own ma must be, I mostly soak in the positive atmosphere and do some not unrelated brainstorming.

Faye was right about my getting busier. I could use some help. I wonder if Cy would like to go into business with me. The local dog-caring scene is exploding. Owners and dogs like me, and same as everybody else, they'll adore Cy. Agatha turned me down, so at least I tried, and if I hire Cy, I'm covered just in case she tries to change her mind. Perfect.

We'd make a killing, in a socially acceptable way. I'm a good bit into my planning when Ma snaps me to attention.

"So, how does that sound to you, Louis?" she says.

"Um, good?" I guess.

"I think it's a great idea," Cy says in my direction. I don't know if he's consciously bailing me out, but that's what he's achieving. "I've already done all the stuff you're coming up to. I did the homeschooling, transitioned to the high school like you'll be doing. I can teach you just fine, seeing as I learned from the best." He gestures toward Ma, who looks mighty pleased at this, and at the mound of sleeping dog crushing her legs.

I'm catching on. Not rapidly but getting there. And it's a sound plan. I could learn some things from Cy. And we could combine the illusion of tutoring with the reality of dog business. *And* get Faye off my academic case for good.

Best of all, it's a good plan because it's an easily undermined plan. Or, if not undermined, certainly bent toward my purposes.

I don't need any more tutoring from anybody. I'm as ready as I'll ever be to hit high school, whether anybody agrees with that assessment or not. Anyway, how hard could it be?

"Great stuff," I say. "Great idea all around."

Ma is smiling in such a sweetly satisfied way, and that alone is just about worth the visit. We're losing her quickly, though. It's about equally a shame to let her drift away from us and to wake up Pierre. But we do, and Cy pats Ma on the hand as he says his goodbye.

"We'll talk about the lessons," she says.

"We will," he says.

• • •

I have new energy as we make our way back home. I let Cy in on my master plan to build up a business empire together. Cy contemplates for a few minutes and then approves of my business plan.

"And the beauty of it is," I say, "you really don't have to sweat the tutoring stuff at all. We'll go through the motions, you and I will get covered in dog hair and money, and my studies . . . will pretty much take care of themselves."

It's Cy's turn to go deep frosty silent for a minute or so.

"No," he says.

"No?" I says.

"No. Here's how it goes. I am very much going to tutor you. In exactly the same way your mother did me. I'm going to do it all her way. From the academics, to the social stuff . . . to the citizenship issues that mean so much to her."

"The *what* issues now?"

"Louis, it's a matter of honor. I intend to carry out your mother's wishes, to the letter and beyond. I'm going to try as hard as I can to make your life as tough as she would if she could. I owe that to her. And to you."

We're nearing the point where our paths diverge. I'm hurrying to get to that point.

"Well," I say, "I think I must be about to break some kind of speed-firing record, but your services are no longer required."

"Okay," he says casually. "It was great while it lasted."

As he and Pierre split off down the road, he calls after me, "Let me know when you change your mind."

13. Plans

I DECIDE MAYBE I CAN MIX AND MATCH THE PARTS OF MA'S plan, my plan, and Cy's plan (even if he doesn't know he's got a plan) into something I can use.

"Faye, I have excellent news," I say as I stand in her doorway. She's making her bed, in that tight way marines do, so that you could bounce a quarter off it. You could probably bounce a marine off it.

"What?" she asks, in her mildly interested way that actually indicates great interest.

"I've made Cy an offer he can't refuse, even though he has attempted to refuse it, but in the end, he'll be joining my dog-walking operation and also pretending to tutor me for school. So you and your mother can stop worrying about me and my schoolwork."

I have to give myself credit here. . . . Okay I don't *have* to but, y'know . . . I pivot and sweep out into the hallway with impeccable timing and style.

"Cy?" she asks in a sort of puppy-yelp. She comes cantering out into the hall and grabs my arm before I reach the kitchen. "What are you *doing*?" she shout-whispers at me, as if Cyrus himself is waiting in the kitchen.

"Whatever do you mean?" I ask, and never have I enjoyed deliciously chewing on a question quite so much. Sometimes it's fun to be a brother.

She punches me hard, straight in the sternum. Sometimes it's painfully fun to be a brother.

"You know I have . . . *feelings* around Cy. I can't function with him around here. I'm only now getting over the whole SAT thing."

"I thought you had . . . *feelings* around Greta Thunberg."

She punches me again, harder. Though maybe the spot's just more tender now.

"Stop limiting my life chances, *Louie*!"

"Listen," I say, "I'd love to do this all day, but I've got a pretty full slate for a Sunday."

I do my pivot-sweep thing again, and man, I'm really honing it. She tries to catch me, but I'm through the kitchen and out the back way just before she can snag me. I think I hear her scratching at the door.

I text Cy.

Listen, maybe I'm right, maybe you're right, maybe my ma is right. But still, we would make an awesome team. Can we have a business meeting?

I expect a big pause. But no.

Sure. Let's do a meet.

Ok. So?

Come to my place.

Oh. Ok?

He tells me where, exactly, and I get a little edgy. But I'm going.

The deal is that I'm to call him when I'm approaching his building, but that turns out not to be necessary. He must've been watching, because he and Pierre are on the path toward the sidewalk at the same time I arrive.

"Hey," I say.

"Hey," he says, and then gestures behind him, to the tunnel that leads to the back side of the apartment complex.

"Where we going?" I ask as I slap Pierre's big, glorious dome.

"To the store," Cy says.

"I didn't know there was a store around back here," I say.

"That's 'cause it's not your store," he says. "Mere wants a few things, for her cookin'. Sweet potatoes, coconut, a few other bits. My mere is an awesome cook, so when she demands ingredients . . . I go get those ingredients. You feel me?"

"I think I do," I say.

"Emelio usually has whatever we need. It's a small shop, but a smart one. He knows what to keep on his shelves."

We round the back corner of the building, toward what appear to be another bunch of apartments. I follow along as Cy heads to the corner of the lot, stopping short of another tunnel that separates his building from another one running perpendicular to it.

"Cy, where are we going?" I ask. "I don't see anything that looks—"

Cy and Pierre don't even break stride as they walk into a ground-floor apartment, without even knocking.

Because it turns out not to be just an apartment.

"Emelio!" Cy calls.

"Pierre!" Emelio calls.

Cy turns to me, "That happens a whole lot. If I'm with P I might as well be invisible."

"Fair enough," I say.

"Fair enough. Hey, Emelio, this is my friend, Louis. Louis, this is Emelio. Also known as The Mayor."

"Nice to meet you, Mayor."

"And you," he says. "Any friend of Pierre's . . ."

Emelio is standing behind what I would call a breakfast bar, if this place was on its off hours and just being an apartment. But since it's on duty, I'd call it a shop counter. There are crowded shelves up and down the wall behind him, a fridge, a tiny stove. "What's on your mind, kid?"

"Sweet potatoes are on my mind, sir. And shredded coconut. And peanut butter—the good stuff with actual peanuts in it and not loaded up with salt and xylitol. That's terrible for the birds. And bread."

With every beat, every demand, Emelio grabs the item off a shelf behind him or from someplace under the counter without even looking. Cy nods at the bag of four sweet potatoes, the packet of coconut, the jar of peanut butter.

"Oh, nah, nah, nah," Cy protests when the white bread

appears. "Not that junk, Emelio. There's more salt in that than in a giant bag of potato chips. And *still* it manages to taste like nothin'. You know if I bring that up to Celia, you and I will both be dead meat. I wanna see something with whole grains and with real seeds right in the obvious there where I can identify them."

Having gotten the proper rise out of Cy, Emelio is laughing as he swaps out the no-good bread for the all-good bread.

"Now, that's what I'm talkin' about," Cy says, embracing the loaf affectionately. He grabs up most of the stuff, gesturing for me to get the peanut butter. I do, and as we head out, Cy calls back, "On the bill, yeah, E?"

"Bill's gettin' kinda puffy," Emelio answers.

"Don't worry," Cy says, allowing me to hold the door for him, "I'm good. Strategizing with my partner here to address that very situation, sir." He's grinning broadly as he heads out the door, and the next customer heads in.

"Where you been?" Cy says to her as she passes him. I continue holding the door for her.

"Around," she says as if she's distracted, or rushed.

She blanks me entirely. Not even a thanks, despite my holding the door. And despite her being Agatha.

I catch up to Cy and Pierre. "You know her?" I ask. "How?"

"I don't *know her* know her. Just like, 'Hi, hello, how are ya' know her. Because she lives in the same building as me."

"Here?" I say a little breathlessly. "She lives *here*?"

His response is flat. "Something wrong with that?"

"No. No, no. It's just, I thought she lived somewhere else is all."

My head is spinning from that, but fortunately, just on the inside. I follow Cy up the stairs to the fourth floor.

"No elevator, then?" I wheeze.

"There is one," he says. "But it doesn't work. I'd say it's broken, but because it always doesn't work, that's its natural condition."

We're walking down the long corridor when it occurs to me. "So, you told Emelio we're in business, so I guess we really are. In business."

He stops and spins in my direction. "Not quite yet. You've obviously passed the Pierre test. But I can't move forward with any plan that doesn't have the Celia stamp of approval. And she's a tougher customer than he is." He pivots once more and throws open the door to the last apartment on the top floor of the building.

She is standing there waiting. A slim woman, about five-five, with silky black hair that's cut pixie-like and hugs her forehead and cheekbones like ivy. Her skin is just a shade lighter than the hair that frames it.

"Celia Toussaint," Cy announces in a big, embarrassing voice, "this is Louis Singletary. Louis, this is Celia. Ma-*ma*."

Hearing my name like that, so soon after being introduced to Emelio, I feel like my circle of acquaintances has about doubled in the last half hour.

"So nice to meet you, Louis," she says, extending her hand.

"My pleasure," I say, and absently hand her the peanut butter. She laughs softly, puts the jar on the counter behind her, and takes my hand warmly in both of hers. She releases me and quickly snags the bread away from her son.

"Would you like a peanut butter sandwich?" she asks me.

"No thank you, ma'am. I ate not too long ago."

"Good," she says as she gets down to the business of making a peanut butter sandwich anyway. I must be gawping at her as she does this, because Cy chuckles and comes up close to inform me that the sandwich is for the birds. Literally.

"There's never enough for them, the poor desperate little things," Ms. Toussaint says as she slathers generous gobs of peanut butter between the two slices of quality grainy bread. Then, just before slapping them together, she pulls down a jar of sunflower seeds from the top of the refrigerator and pours a load of them over the whole thing. She takes the impressive slab across the room, to the window, where she opens it up and places the treat into a sort of cage-like, sandwich-shaped feeder dangling like a hanging basket beside the window. There is a scrubby, thinning old ash tree stretching up past the window. It sounds like it houses a whole aviary of feathered fans of peanut butter. She closes the window and brushes her hands off, as several birds swoop right in on the meal.

"I used to keep canaries, back in Haiti," she says proudly. "Caught them myself, with wooden traps and cages I made personally. This isn't the same, of course, but it's satisfying to be able to feed the homeless birds here, living out in the cold and all."

This is, to me, a fairly great and unusual story. I'm impressed, though Cy has obviously heard it all before.

"Saint Cecelia," he says, cackling.

"You," she snaps, "have some root vegetables to chop. Off to the sink with ya, mister."

He doesn't hesitate on his way to the kitchen sink, and I don't blame him.

Ms. Toussaint takes a seat at the small table on the non-kitchen side of the counter. She pats the seat next to her, and I oblige. Pierre works himself into the bit of space on the floor between us. She instantly puts her bare feet up on his back, and he leans heavily into his job as ottoman.

She opens strong. "So, I hear you're a momma's boy."

"Cyyy," I sigh loudly.

"No, no," she says, "I mean that as a compliment. Just so happens I raised one of those myself."

Cy whine time. "Ceeel-yaa."

Moving right along. "So, dogs," she says.

"Dogs," I repeat, adding a bobblehead nod.

"What kind of dog do you have?"

"I don't have one, actually," I say. "I suppose they're all sort of my dogs. I love them all. Basically, my flock."

"Pierre's not yours," Cy calls.

"Except Pierre," I say. "I'm kinda like a parish priest."

Ms. Toussaint scowls at me so sharply I get a pain in the middle of my forehead.

Cy knows without even seeing. He appears at the counter, flopping himself over it to reassure her. "Celia," he says, "it's not like that. Nothing religious about our operation. Nothing culty."

"Good," she says, pointing a serious finger at me. "Dogs are pure beings. They got no need for no church."

"Yes, ma'am," I warble. "Neither do I, so we're good."

She smiles broadly at me. "Yes, we are. We're good." She reaches both hands across the table toward me, and though this feels strange to me, I reach across and link hands with her.

It immediately stops feeling strange. Except for the sudden rush, of thoughts and feelings of my own mother's thin, warming hands. I'm getting a little wobbly with it, worried I might crack, when my phone rings.

I look up from Ms. Toussaint's hands and into her clear eyes with my watery ones. "I don't wish to be rude," I say, "but may I? My phone doesn't ring often."

"Off with ya," she says, flinging my hands away dramatically but giggling at the same time.

I head toward the door as I answer. Cy looks over at me and I give him the standard just-a-minute wave. I'm out in the hall when I say my hello.

The response is not a hello, but, "I suppose you're wondering..."

"Ah, what do you mean?"

"Okay then, see ya..."

"All right, yes, I'm wondering. I'm way wondering, as a matter of fact."

"Right. I'm guessing you're in the building?"

"Yeah. I'm visiting."

"My, haven't you become the social butterfly. Well, when you're done, I'm in 314. Feel free to stop by. If you're not all socialized out."

I only get one *ha* into my *ha-ha* before she hangs up.

When I come back into the apartment, sweet potatoes are simmering on the stovetop, and Cy is simmering on the couch. Though just for show. I think.

"I invite you to my house," he says, "and the first thing you do is take a call, out in the hallway. I just don't know about your generation. Rude."

I don't have a lot to work with here, but I give it a go. "It wasn't the *first* thing I did, actually."

I move to take the seat next to him on the couch, and he quickly pats the cushion and whistles, bringing Pierre bounding into the spot.

"It's no wonder you got no friends," he says.

This again?

"Now who's being rude?" Ms. Toussaint says. She comes over and shoves first Pierre and then Cy off the couch. "Mr. Pierre, Mr. Cyrus, you know the rules, no dogs on my sofa." She sits down and does the cushion pat for me to sit, but without the whistle. "Dog. Just like his father," she says.

Oh, I could warm to this. "Is he?"

"Not in the slightest," she says happily. "If he was, he wouldn't be here, that's for sure. Cyrus's dad disappeared years ago, back to his home planet."

"Maine," Cy adds. "We think. But never mind him."

"I never do," she adds.

"Who was so important you had to take that call?" Cy asks.

"Oh," I say, "that was Agatha. We saw her downstairs?"

"Ah, so that's her name. I only knew her as 'hello.' You got a little crush there, boy," Celia says.

"No," I answer, quickly and emphatically. Way too quickly and emphatically.

Ms. Toussaint laughs heartily and throws an arm over my shoulders. "Ha," she says. "I wasn't even there, and I can tell it's the truth."

"Shoulda seen it, Celia," her son cackles. "He could barely hold the door open, his knees were wobbling so much."

Killing me. They're killing me here. I should probably hate it more.

"Oh, stop now, Cyrus," she says, pulling me closer.

"Yes, Cyrus, stop now," I say, before standing up. "I have to go, anyway. It was nice to meet you, Ms. Toussaint."

"Call me Celia," she says, "and the pleasure was all mine. Now that you boys are in business together, I hope to see more of you. Come around anytime."

"Thank you very much . . . Celia."

I pat Pierre on the head, wave silently at my partner, and just about make it to the door without incident.

"Where you have to be so suddenly?" Cy calls, barely controlling his laughter.

I immediately shave about four years off my age by calling back, "I don't have to tell you *anything*," before barreling out.

Apartment 314 is one flight down and a couple of very long corridors away. Just like when I first came up with Cy, I notice very few signs of life. Maybe one door out of every four has some conversation or the sound of a TV coming out of it. Up until I ran into Cy I didn't even realize people still lived here at all.

I knock at door 314. A dog barks.

Agatha opens the door just wide enough to present her face. And it's quite a small face. "You have a dog?" I ask.

"I told you that."

"Oh right," I say, "the three-legged dog . . . that lives in your bedroom . . . in the mansion . . . and that has the same name as me. Forgive me if I didn't take all that straight to the bank, Aggie."

"I never said all that," she says. The dog barks again.

"Are you gonna let me in?" I ask. "You did invite me."

She's exasperating me already, and I let her know it with a big huff.

"Why do you lie?" I say.

"I don't," she says. "But what's the truth ever done for anybody anyway?"

The dog barks again. "Two of the three of us would like me to come inside," I say. "Do you want me to just go?"

Her suddenly troubled expression tells me she doesn't. Instead she throws the door open wide.

Standing behind her is a three-legged dog.

"You're kidding me," I say, walking past the girl to get to the dog. "What's Billie doing here?"

"Um, this isn't Billie."

"Right, I forgot you already had a three-legged dog. This is Lewis, then? Same name as me, only different spelling?"

"Sheesh. Men. You really do make everything about you. *Lois*. I said Lois. I told you, her name is Lois. Get over yourself already."

Lois seems tentatively pleased to see me. I walk up to her and stroke her as much as she will allow. She really is a special being, whatever her name is.

"How'd you get her to come home with you?" I ask as unprovocatively as I can.

"Just made sure she knew the decision was up to her. That nobody was forcing her to. And I played along with her game. She ran from me, but just because she wanted to be chased."

"You chased her?" I say. "And . . . you caught her? This sleek racing-dog-type creature?"

"Ah, come on," she says, "poor thing's only got three legs."

"But look at those legs," I marvel. "I couldn't catch her if she only had one."

She reaches out and pats me on the head. "I know," she says sadly.

"You must be really fast," I say.

She nods several times rapidly. "Yes," she says, "I am. I often thought about this, that if I had friends, they'd call me Gazelle. Wouldn't that be cool?"

I nearly double over with how sad that makes my stomach. I want to tell her, no, this is why you *don't* want friends, because then nobody could ever make you feel this feeling.

But I decide to take it in a different direction. "Aggie, I promise I will call you Gazelle at least once a week if you promise not to say anything like that again."

"Okay," she chirps, sweetly stabbing my stomach once more.

Lois-Lewis-Billie struck me as a creature who knew what she wanted and what she didn't want. And I figured she didn't want to come out of the woods and settle down with anybody. I knew from the get-go that this dog was special. It had to take somebody special to bring her home.

"It's good," Agatha says, coming close to bump me aside and gently caress Lois's torpedo skull. "This is really good. It's *so* good. It's so sweet."

This is an awful lot of friending for one day. I'm squirming with how overwhelmed it's making me. But it's great, too. For both of them. They're amazing, individually and especially together. This might be the rightest thing I ever saw up close.

"Should I go?" I ask, hoping hard that yes is the answer.

"No, you shouldn't," she says, taking me by the hand and leading me down a dark hallway toward a lighter living room. Lois bounces along beside her, natural as anything.

There's a big living room window that looks out over some scrabbly grass toward the same tree that Cy's apartment looks out at. The room itself has two very different green armchairs set on opposite sides of an oval, raw-pine coffee table that smells powerfully of coffee. Very bitter coffee.

We sit and look at each other for a while. We take turns patting the dog, and the dog takes turns indulging each of us.

"So, who else lives here?" I finally ask.

"My parents," she says flatly.

"Oh, okay, good," I say. "All of you together, that's nice."

"Not exactly," she says. "They're not together. But that's the good part. They split, and I got joint custody. Meaning, this is the place, and I live here all the time, and they come and go, either him or her here, but never together. Thank god."

"I'm sorry," I say.

"Why? You didn't do anything. Did you?"

"Um, no, I don't think so. But . . . how do you keep it all straight, with the coming and going?"

She shrugs.

I do something like a shrug, which is actually a spine shiver.

"I'm fine," she says. "As long as they're not both here at the same time. I can't take that. I bug out whenever that happens."

"Bug out? Where do you stay?"

She shrugs again.

Somebody's at the door. Not a knock, but somebody coming in. Agatha looks slightly panicked. She grabs my hand and scuttles down the hall, with Lois right beside us. We reach her door in a few seconds and are quickly inside.

"Who is it?" I say.

"Don't know," she whispers. "One of them. Doesn't matter, really."

I'm shocked, shaking, no idea what I'm supposed to do here.

"I should go," I say.

"You shouldn't," she says. "Not now."

"Um, when, then?" I say.

"Tomorrow?" she says more softly than she's ever said anything.

"Excuse me?" I say.

"Stay with me. Please?"

"I can't do that."

"Sure you can."

"In this room? Your room? Like, overnight and everything?"

"All that, yeah."

"No."

"It's fine. They won't come in here if they know you're here. We'll make noise just to be sure."

"No way."

"Why not?"

"Because," I say. "It's ... not right. It's just not."

"Right and wrong. Huh. That's funny."

"Is it?"

I'm finding myself getting all tensed up because of this, and I'm not entirely sure what it's all about. But when I hear another door slam in the apartment, I panic and make my break for it.

"I thought you were my friend," she calls after me, and it feels like she has shot me through the back with an arrow.

It's not enough to slow my escape, though.

I almost get away. I make it down all the stairs and out the door to the footpath toward the street.

"Hey, *friend*," Aggie shouts.

Bagged, I stop short and spin in her direction. She comes stomping up to me with Lois on a leash. Not a leash, exactly, but a belt buckled loosely around her slender neck. She comes up and forces the belt into my hands.

"Nobody would have minded if you stayed," she says. "In my world, anybody sleeps in anybody's room, and nobody cares. *But* I never got permission to bring home a dog. For that, there would be . . . penalties. So if you still want to be even a little bit my friend, you take Lois home temporarily, while I smooth this over. Deal?"

"Deal," I say as fast as a person can say *deal*.

"Temporarily," she snarls, jabbing a finger in my face before crouching down and caressing the dog's. Then she spins and heads back to whatever she's heading back to.

14. Amos

DEALMAKING HAS BECOME A BIG DEAL AROUND HERE lately. I have Lois, *temporarily*. Faye has swooped in and half stolen her away from me anyway, in another defeat for the patriarchy.

"I told you she didn't smell rich," Faye says as I hand her foster dog over, along with the story that came with it. "I love this dog," she says, with a death hug around Lois's swanny neck. "Also, I think I like Aggie better now too."

Feels like we're winning all over. I pull out my phone and call Cy. But he's one step ahead of me, as usual, and I hear his phone ringing right outside my front door. His ringtone is the "Hallelujah" chorus from the *Messiah*.

"Hi," I say, answering the doorbell-phone I just now invented.

He waves me away, like he's on a very important call.

I hang up on him, tugging him by the arm into the house. I turn my suddenly red-hot management skills in the direction of my business partner and try to manage him off the job of tutoring me.

"Can't you just, like, not do it?" I propose. "I really don't need more tutoring between now and the start of school. I know my stuff."

"I can't lie to your ma," he says.

"Fine. Then could you maybe figure out how to tutor me in a way that I don't notice you're doing it?"

"Hmm," he says. "Interesting. You mean, like, educate you and fool you at the same time?"

"Exactly," I say.

He looks me up and down, as if that's even necessary or enlightening. "Yeah, I'm pretty sure I can do that."

I'm fairly certain I've been insulted there. I'm equally sure I don't care.

Truth is, Ma just really wants me to be more like Cy all over. We don't need math and science lessons to make that happen.

Cy and I are a fine team. We make one great four-legged beast, as much as any of the ones we care for so expertly. Maybe that's why they like us so much. My new partner might be a little too committed to Ma's goody-two-shoes-citizen approach to things, but he's giving me valuable insight into life on the outside, moving from homeschooling into the real world, and from the minor leagues into high school society. All of which I'm sorely unprepared for, so these could be considered remedial classes.

It also helps that we can weave these lessons in and out of the working days, so that I'm getting paid while simultaneously absorbing his words of wisdom.

And he's got plenty of those.

"And on the seventh day," he announces as he emerges from my bathroom, "he took a monster dump. And behold, it was very good."

I sigh at Cy. I do that a lot, since the more I work with him the more I realize Cy is a wise guy. And he seems to like making me sigh.

"What's that, like from a song or something?" I ask.

"Or something," he says. "Except that the 'or something' is only *the Holy Bible*! Book of Genesis," he says with great, big fatness, like I'm supposed to fall over backward.

Cy likes God a lot. I have no reason to believe the feeling isn't mutual. That doesn't make either one of them a bad guy.

"So," I say, "then it probably is in a song, somewhere."

He makes like he's pondering my words, which he does frequently. The *makes like* part, since I don't get the feeling he ponders me much at all.

"You could be right there, Lou."

I'm not warming up to the Lou thing. But the Cy thing can get away with stuff like that, and he knows it.

It's eventually made clear to me that the seventh-day reference is due to the fact that we are, unusually, working on a Sunday. That's how good business has gotten. Even people who have the time to spend more of it with their own animals are deferring to us. That's how beloved we are. Cy's been making constant references to this fact, as he's not a huge fan of working on the Sabbath (God's frowning upon it and all), though he's not *not* a fan of collecting the extra dough.

We've each completed our separate morning rounds and

are now convening for a sort of brunch deal (I don't care for that term much, but it is Sunday, and at least that stops you from having to decide on either breakfast or lunch items, which I don't like to have to do) before we set out on afternoon appointments together. We're tossing around potential names for our business. Cy likes Cyberdogs, while I favor Dogs Love Louis.

"Name for what?" asks Faye as she ambles into the kitchen with Lois at her hip. They've very quickly become a unit.

"For our business," Cy says. "Hiya, Faye."

Cy doesn't get a *hiya* in return. It's not that she's impolite. Cy makes her a little wobbly under normal circumstances, so no-warning Cy, at her kitchen table, on a Sunday, leaves her *hiya* totally and uncharacteristically broken.

"Hiya, Cy," Cy says, helping her along with a little *come to me, come to me* hand gesture.

"Hiya, Cy," she parrots, followed by an involuntary whispered repetition of "Hiya, hiya, Cy . . ."

Lois responds to the hand gesture the way most creatures do. She comes right up to Cy. Faye doesn't object, making moon-eyes instead.

It's not often I would describe my sister as cute. But now . . . okay, no, *almost*, but still no.

Brunch today comes in the form of burgers, my specialty, as this is the only meal I ever make. I'm so expert at it, a diner couldn't do a better, or quicker, job. Bacon double cheeseburgers with Swiss on top and bottom, Muenster between the patties, and the whole thing on a seeded brown bun. Dill pickle spears and curly fries. Caesar dressing, barbecue sauce, and honey mustard—your choice, but if you don't use all three, you're extremely sad. I already had three of these meals laid out because I count on the fact that my sister can sniff out bacon, beef, and Cyrus from the lower forty and be here before the plates hit the table.

We're all three digging into my frankly world-class burgers when another scent enters the room.

Ike.

You know when you get Novocain at the dentist and then all afternoon everything you eat tastes like the same fuzzy, furry nothing? Ike instantly does that to my amazing burger.

"What are you doing here?" Faye asks.

"Nice to see you, too, Faybe-baby. I'm here to go out bluefishing with my father. I was kinda hoping you guys would be coming out with us."

Lois, who has flattened herself out half under the table by Faye's feet, rumbles out the low growl of a much bigger creature.

"Whoa," Ike says, taking a couple of steps back. "Where's the rest of this dog? And what's its problem?"

"That's the whole dog," Faye says in a bored voice, "and I guess she's just a shrewd judge of character."

"You shouldn't judge," Ike says, pointing an unwise finger close to Lois's snout.

The curl of the dog's lip suggests the finger could soon become her brunch.

"The man fishes all week," I say. "Why is he going out on a Sunday?"

"He's got a big charter group he's taking out, and he

invited me along. I hope it's a bachelor party. All that vomit brings the blues running like mad."

"Sounds appetizing," Cy says.

"Most delicious fish in the world," Ike says. He walks up and offers his hand to Cy. "Do I know you?"

He knows him. We all know he knows him.

"Cy," Cy says as they shake.

"Sigh. And pant, and gasp, and swoon," Ike says with a laugh. "I'm happy to meet you, too. See what I did there?"

"Everybody sees what you did," Faye says. "And like with everything else you do, everyone wishes you didn't."

Dad steps into the room, dressed for seafaring. "Thought I heard the Big One out here," he says.

Faye and I groan together. "Daaaad," she says, "you promised to stop calling him 'the Big One.'"

Ike could hardly be happier. "Don't hate me 'cause I'm beautiful," he says.

"It's only because you're ugly that we don't hate you more," I say.

"I don't know about you," Faye says, "but I couldn't possibly hate him more."

"Stop hating your brother," Dad scolds us. Dad couldn't properly scold if the scolding police kicked in the door and forced him to at gunpoint.

And we don't hate our brother. Simulated hate is fun and healthy, though.

It's often the visitor's task to introduce sense into a situation. "Is it always like this here?" Cy asks.

"Not always," Faye says, "just since Ma—"

Since Ma.

She's right, of course. It's all gone a little wibbly-wobbly since Ma ... what? What did she do, exactly?

Faye had certainly intended a complete sentence there. Caught herself up short, however, and at the same time took the wind out of everybody's sails.

"She'll be home soon, guys," Dad says as if he's a stranger in a big city, asking for directions. Same way he always says it.

"Sure she will," says Cy, the guy who knows the least about it, but who has us all listening to him anyway. We're wide-open to somebody stepping in and making sense of things at this point.

Floor's yours, friend.

"Nobody else coming?" asks Dad as he and the Big One scuttle out the front door. They seem like they'd scuttle away faster if any of us said yes.

We get back to eating, but not to talking about Ma.

Post-brunch, there's a Weimaraner. He's nuts. They're all nuts. Like Dalmatians and Irish setters. Gorgeous, elegant creatures with legs that go on forever. But mentally troubled.

Ghostly, silvery, velvety blue coat. Steely eyes that can't comprehend the notion of eye contact.

The Weimaraner doesn't care about any of that. Doesn't want to know.

His name is Fahrvergnügen.

According to his owners/keepers/associates/pals ... most importantly, my paymasters ... that's German for the joy of driving. I don't believe Fahrvergnügen does actually drive, but if he wanted to, I would let him. I can't imagine trying to take the keys away from this fella.

I call him Nugen.

He calls me Rrrrrr.

I accompany my new business partner to Fahrvergnügen's house to introduce him to the family. Once we get through those social niceties and the three of us are back out on the sidewalk, we make our plan. I need to backtrack a couple of blocks to collect old pal Amos, while Cy and Nugen get acquainted, and we all then meet down at the riverside, where the dogs can do that romping dog thing dogs are so good at.

"Nah," Cy says.

"Nah?" I say.

"I'm not in a river mood," he says.

"Are you not?" I ask, a little surprised at my associate's attitude. "It's a little soon in the partnership for you to be going all diva on me, dontcha think there, Cyrus? What kind of mood *are* you in, may I ask?"

"Cemetery."

"Cemetery."

"Cemetery. I'm in a cemetery kind of mood."

"So, less diva, more ghoul," I say.

"You could say that," he says.

I have no problem with that. It's a big bruise of a sky

hanging over us today, threatening rain, but probably an idle threat as far as I can taste. Graveyard weather. I like a good cemetery as much as anyone, and ours is a pretty good cemetery. Fahrvergnügen is equally pleased with the choice, springing up and down on his two front pistons as if he is well aware of the decision and is quite looking forward to unearthing himself a nice crunchy human femur. If you had ever seen Nugen forage, you would agree this is a totally feasible outcome.

"Right, it's a date. Amos and I will meet you two guys at the cemetery in about fifteen minutes."

"Right," Cy says, "see you there."

"Grrr-wheeze," Nugen says, straining on the leash and dragging Cy up the road.

I have it timed almost perfectly for Amos's two o'clock constitutional. It being the weekend, Old Man Dan will have taken him for a leisurely stroll right after breakfast, and the two of them should have spent the hours since just lolling in the way Sundays were meant for. Amos isn't altogether enthusiastic about his longer walks these days, but given enough time to recharge, he's still a cheerie chappie and good company once he hits the pavement. Dan, on the other hand, is a one-walk-a-day man. Which is good for business, good for me.

As I make my way down the short, paved walkway that runs alongside Old Man Dan Cottage toward the kitchen door around the side, I'm pretty sure I hear the familiar snuffling, chuffing, heaving whistle-sigh that's Amos's theme tune.

I knock on the door. Wait. Knock some more, and then some more. The Amos noises keep seeping out of the kitchen, so still I wait, but neither man nor beast appears. I lean up close to the frosted-pane glass of the door and can just about make out a moving shadowy something across the room. When I knock again and get more nothing, I gently work the door open, calling both residents of the house while I enter as honorably as an intruder can.

"Dan?" I say, as I peek around the door and now see him clearly. He's on the floor.

His back is to the low cupboard where Amos's manky food is kept. The bowl is there, full, next to Dan's right hip, and flush up against his left is Amos.

Those Amos noises I heard were coming out of Dan. Amos has got no noises left. His one eye is held half-open by the way it's pressed up to the black canvas belt of Old Man Dan's crusty tan chinos. Amos's tongue dangles down out of the side of his mouth, all the way to the linoleum floor, looking like it's tethering him there.

Old Man Dan's crying, gasping for air as desperately as all those fish he landed over all those years. I go all panicky, looking around the room like a clueless numbskull, for something, for what? Anything that will make this in any way better. Like there is a kitchen appliance, some utensils, a solid, tangible anything that will help Dan to breathe. That will help Amos to breathe.

To my sickened surprise, there is no such something.

Old Man Dan keeps on wheezing and whistling, his

strange deranged tribute to the Old Dog Amos, who cannot do it himself anymore. He looks up at me with an expression I don't recognize, with bulging eyes I can't believe belong to a still-living being. He holds out one hand to me—because the other hand is not leaving his dog's side—holds out his hand turned upward, fingers spread wide, like he's reaching for something I'm offering, like there's something I'm supposed to be giving him. But I've got nothing. I've got nothing.

"Dan," I say. "Mr. Evans," I say. "Oh, Mr. Evans, I'm so sorry," I say.

As I back out the kitchen door again.

"You did *what?*" Cy demands when I run up to him, with Nugen frolicking amid the headstones and bones.

"I left," I say, realizing with the sound of the words in the air just how pathetic those words are. "I just . . . left. I didn't know what to do. I was . . . I felt like . . ."

Like I was five. That's how I felt. Like I had lost my parents at the beach on a sweltering Labor Day and all I could do was run wildly through the Coppertoney legs of ten thousand strangers, calling for my ma, for my ma, for my ma.

Sort of like I did on my trip just now to meet up with my friend. And crying, just the same. And calling for my ma.

"Are you crying, Louis?" Cy says.

"Not anymore," I say.

"Lou," he says, both sympathetic and not. "Dogs die, y'know, man."

"Well," I say, all of five, all over again, "they shouldn't."

He gives me roughly six seconds to compose myself.

He hooks Fahrvergnügen back up to the leash, grabs me hard enough to nearly dislocate my shoulder, then hauls the two of us out of the graveyard.

"You're going back there, pal. Now." The *now* part was probably unnecessary.

There are two dog walkers standing in Old Man Dan's kitchen. There are two dogs, one of them breathing.

Fahrvergnügen and Cyrus stand erect by Dan's kitchen door, like a couple of centurions. After a sharp elbow nudge from Cy, I stumble forward toward the inhabitants of this house, who are exactly where I left them.

Dan is all cried out. Amos is all everythinged out.

With no other thoughts in my head and my escape route thoroughly blocked, I do the thing I can do. I step up, and fall down, into the spot on the floor to the right of Dan, while he still clings to Amos on his left.

"He was a beautiful boy, Mr. Evans," I say.

There is no known measure by which Amos was beautiful. But still, he was.

"He was, wasn't he?" Dan says. He finally leans away from ol' Amos and into me. "My boy was a beautiful boy."

I open my mouth to say more but find that there is no more.

Cy steps up briskly, along with Fahrvergnügen. I know that Nugen is thinking about all those delicious Amos bones, almost available, almost there for the gnarling. But dog remains almost as dignified as the man. He stands rigid, at attention, at Cy's side.

"He was beautiful," Cy says, extending hands to me and Dan, then hauling us up off the floor. He settles, then, to a dignified whisper. "You have a spot, Mr. Evans? For Amos to rest? I'm guessing you have picked out a spot?"

Old Man Dan goes silent and noddy. Nodding, nodding, nodding, he leads us out the side door and around to the square patch of back lawn and the tight little corner that's been waiting for Amos. For some while. Then all of us, an honor guard of three dog guys and one dog, escort Amos—who shockingly smells better in death than in life—to the spot. We dig and we prepare and we inter him into that spot of earth. And then we're done.

Nobody talks. We make the place neat, then neater. Nobody talks.

Old Man Dan doesn't even look at us as he stands over Amos's grave and waits.

Eventually, we get it, and we go.

We're close to Nugen's house when I finally make a sound.

"It was good you were there," I say. "Thanks."

Cy goes walking up the path to return the dog. He waves me away toward home.

15. Brothers and Keepers

THE WEEK AFTER AMOS'S DEATH IS A LONG ONE. I DON'T walk dogs so much as drag them. But the clouds lift gradually, and my smarter self recognizes that the only real response to dog-grief is, of course, dogs.

There are two sheepdogs, Wilbur and Orville. They're identical twins, but only on the outside. Named after the famous aviator Wright brothers. That's misleading, though. Orville is no Wright. He's seriously wrong.

They're still young, just a year old, though they look like mobile haystacks. The owners recognize the personality divide and have switched over to a double leash that keeps them yoked closely together. In theory, this is to encourage an attitude meld between them over time. I've seen some evidence of this, since Wilbur is more of a jerk than he was before, but we're still hoping for better results.

Barking at everything and nothing, trying to pick fights constantly, knocking over trash cans for snacks, and tearing up public property for kicks probably sounds like a lot of fun to a certain type of beast, but it gets right on the nerves of absolutely everybody else. I have a new appreciation for what my parents went through raising Ike.

Wilbur would probably be all right off the leash sometimes, but because Orville can't do it, he can't do it.

"Life isn't even fair to *dogs*," Cy says as we walk away from the Wright brothers' house.

"No, it isn't," I snarl.

It's a wasted snarl, since he doesn't even seem to notice. The word *seem* there is important, because he might, and probably does, recognize my mood. But he's an expert at bringing the light and lightness. Whether it belongs or not.

Speaking of what doesn't belong, Cy doesn't. Not now, anyway. It's two dogs, one leash, early-early before there's much going on in the world to bother us at all—other than Sir Cyrus. The dogs' masters are traveling on business and are insistent that their hairy handfuls get to romp in the sunrise every day. When I say that *romp in the sunrise* stuff is an actual quote, I have painted an accurate picture of the Wright brothers' family life.

Truth is, I love the sunrise romping business right after breakfast. Solid food and solitude, that's my idea of a complete and ideal morning, and while canine companionship doesn't get in the way of that, the human version definitely does.

There's not even anything for Cy to do. He's not getting paid, either. He's just here, for the fun of it, or whatever.

Or whatever. Whatever could whatever even be?

The question must be on my face as I walk along trying

to puzzle him out, because I suddenly find him grinning at me and waving as if I'm far away.

"You're a lot quieter in the morning," he says obliviously, as we march up the road toward the soccer field.

"Oh," I say, "um, yeah, I guess."

There are no specific instructions for the sheepdogs, which means there are none for us, either. Just stay out for a long time, tire them out as much as that's possible, and avoid having them interact too much with their peers, in order to avoid "incidents." The soccer field at this hour is as good a place as any for incident avoidance.

Summer is tumbling toward fall, my favorite time of year. The early-morning sunshine is just starting to join the game, gentle warming coming along with gentle rays. Nothing's too bright yet, too warm yet. Nothing's too anything yet. It's all just exactly enough, and if Cy were not tagging along and chattering, the birds would be providing all the audio. Pretty much perfection.

Cy's not so bad, actually. It's not quite as sweet as silence, but his conversation is usually interesting, and he basically never says anything stupid. How many fellow walkers can you say that about?

"You beginning to get nervous about starting school?" he asks as we step off the pavement and onto the edge of the dewy grass.

"Nope," I say firmly, while I pull hard on the reins of the dogs. The sudden appearance of the wide-open field has launched them into their hounds-of-hell imitation. They're strong, and I have to lean all the way back, like I'm clinging to a tug-of-war rope.

"Huh," he says, "I didn't figure you to be the cucumber-cool type."

"No cucumbers involved," I say coolly. "You asked if I was beginning to get nervous. The answer's no, because the beginning was about two months ago."

"Ah," he says, drifting behind and grabbing my shoulders to help me contain the dogs. "I see. Well, remember, you've got me there to keep an eye on you. Lucky you. I wish I had me when I was a freshman."

"Lucky me," I say sarcastically, because a dude absolutely has to be sarcastic in that spot, or else things could get soppy. It's baked into the *guy pie*, as my dad would put it. The sarcasm itself was a lie, even if the words were true. Lucky me, true enough.

Orville and Wilbur get suddenly all excited, barking and bounding forward, dragging me along as if this were the Iditarod sled race on grass. I can see what they're after but can't immediately make out what it is. Cy pulls up alongside me and then races past all of us to get to it.

It's a person. Crashed out, facedown, with what looks like a bicycle broken in half and folded around him. Cy rushes up to him, rolls him over, and starts quizzing him.

"You all right?" Cy asks anxiously.

"I'm fine," the guy says, slowly rising to a sitting position.

"Are you hurt? Your face is all covered in dirt. Did you land on your face?"

"I'm fine," the guy repeats, only more annoyed this time.

"He says he's fine," I say, already wanting to move on.

"Just because he says he's fine doesn't mean he's fine," Cy snaps at me.

"Ah, I think that's exactly what it means," I say.

"He might have a concussion," Cy says. "You might have a concussion, pal."

The guy tries to get up, but Cy helpfully forces him back to the ground.

"*You* might have a concussion," the guy growls.

"I'm not the one who fell on his face," Cy says.

"Not yet, you're not," the guy says, shoving Cy's hands away and getting to his feet.

As this little interaction plays itself out, I do something I'm known to do, something I'm accomplished at. I walk away.

Despite its bad reputation, walking away can be a noble act.

The bike-crash guy may look woozy and wobbly. He may smell like the dumpster behind my local Irish bar. He may be covered in far more dirt than one bike crash could have given him.

But he says he's fine. If he says he's fine, who's to say he's not?

Cy's to say, that's who.

The dogs and I are halfway across the soccer field when the guy yells, "Just leave me *alone*, will you?" I turn to see.

"But look at you," Cy says. "You're a mess from that crash."

"I look exactly the way I did before I crashed. But thanks." He remounts the bike.

"Sorry," Cy says. "I didn't mean that. Lemme help you."

Just then the guy crashes again. It's as if the whole bike just breaks into two halves and the guy goes over the handlebars and onto his face. It's painful even to watch from a distance. Cy's rushing to help, but the guy's not having it. He seems to fear Cy's helpfulness more than any jeopardy he might be in. As he hurriedly gathers himself up and continues on, I find myself thinking, *Go, guy, go!*

The go guy goes, about another six feet before crashing in the identical, painful, sad fashion as before.

As he falls on the bike, and the bike falls on him, and they wrestle each other on the ground, I realize: he's riding a fold-up mountain bike. The kind that collapses at a big hinge in the center of the frame. And the lock that holds it firmly in riding position appears to be broken. I believe you're not supposed to ride them when that's the case.

Wilbur and Orville realize what an absurd situation this is. They turn and head in the direction of where Cy and Guy are having words, the dogs hoping, no doubt, to talk sense into them. As with most things O&W, I follow along semi-helplessly.

As we get there, Cy has switched to scolding mode. I'm acquainted with this mode.

"Well, maybe you shouldn't have stolen it in the first place."

"I didn't steal it," the guy says. "It was just lying there on the ground."

"Well, maybe it was dumped there because it's useless."

"It's not useless," the guy says. "You're useless." He punctuates his bold statement with one more dramatic launching of the bike version of the scarecrow from *The Wizard of Oz*.

Followed by one more immediate face-plant.

This time, when the guy gets up, very slowly, blood is streaming down from his nose. I try to make out just who he is in there. Because of the filth of him, and the injuries, the defensiveness and the final embarrassment that has him counting the blades of grass on the soccer field up close, it's all but impossible to tell. He could be my age. He could be Cy's age. He could be my age plus Cy's age. He could be me+Cy+10 for all I know.

He doesn't pick the bike back up. He likewise doesn't lift his eyes from the ground. He takes three strong strides in Cy's direction, till his forehead bumps Cy's nose. Still, he doesn't look up.

The dogs are straining, growling, bouncing, and pulling toward the guy. They want to intervene, and I want to let them.

"You got any dough?" the guy says low. Still not looking up.

Cy stabs his hands down deep into his pockets, digging and fishing.

"Cy, no," I say. The dogs growl the same thing, in their way. "You're being robbed, man. Don't let him . . . We're here with you. The dogs . . ."

Cy pulls out everything he can find, hands it over to the guy.

"Shut up, Lou," he says. "I'm not being robbed."

Without a word, and without another look, the guy takes the money, steps over the bike, and hobbles away, very much like a guy who has been in five, or six, or ten bike crashes already this early in the day.

It should be a good thing that Cy now doesn't feel like talking a lot. That's what I wanted, right? Right?

Right, except wrong. It feels wrong enough that I find myself trying to draw him into conversation.

"Do you do that stuff all the time?" I ask as we're pulled across the field toward some invisible mass of something or somebody. Though the dogs appear to have identified the mass and clearly want it.

"What stuff?" Cy asks.

"You know, all that 'helping everybody' stuff."

Despite the fact that he looks, and sounds, like he's not listening to me at all, he somehow manages to answer. Ish.

"I suppose I do *my* stuff as often as you do *your* stuff."

"And my stuff would be . . . ?"

"Nothing."

"Ah," I say. "Very clever."

"Well, Louis, I don't think I could do what you do. Just turning away from people in need like that guy."

"I don't think that guy thought he was a person in need."

He looks me dramatically up and down, head to toe to head again, and says, "People in need don't always think they're in need."

He's really winding me up now, and I'm sure he knows it.

I don't really have the skills to deal with this, and I'm pretty sure he knows this, too. So I go with mimicking his up-and-down look and saying, "Maybe *you're* a person in need."

Establishing for good that I was indeed not prepared, Cy says possibly the last thing I expected. "Well, maybe I *am*."

So, then, what does a guy do in this situation?

No, really, I need to know.

Cy grabs my shoulder, there in the very center of the field, and he plunks me right down there on the ground. I sit cross-legged—I didn't even know I could do that anymore. He sits the same way across from me. Wilbur and Orville relax around us, sort of grazing in the grass, as if they're more sheep than sheepdog.

"I'm looking forward to school," he says. "I love my ma to bits, but I need to get out and be someplace else. School is good. You're gonna like it."

I think, look at the convincing expression on his face. "I expect to," I say.

"Labor Day's coming up," he says. "Always been my favorite holiday. Summer's just . . . nothing. Happy to be done with it. I like getting back into the world. Family's good, but they're supposed to be behind you. The rest of the world needs to be in front of you."

"Huh," I say. "I guess I never thought about it like that."

We sit for a bit. The weather's perfect. The dogs, serene. The grass is just after-dewy aromatic.

"Well, helping you think is an important part of my job description."

"Yeah?" I say. "Well, then I *think* that you'll *think* it's a positive development when I tell you that there's a freshman orientation coming up at the school, and after serious deliberation I have decided *not* to *not* go."

He stares at me for maybe an hour. "I'm no expert," he finally says, "but I figure if you use fewer words to say stuff, you'll ultimately live longer."

The immense satisfaction I feel at that reaction is only slightly dimmed at the ringing of my phone, then dimmed slightly more to see that it's my brother.

"Hello," I say, but I don't mean it.

"I came by the house, but you're not here," Ike says.

"Yeah, I noticed," I say. "I'm with me right now, as a matter of fact."

Cy splutters out an exaggerated laugh.

"What the hell's going on? You used to always be here. Where are you now?"

"Not telling you," I say.

"Fine," he says, and I hate that he can do this to me, but with a few stupid words he can make the ground beneath my feet tremble. "I'll just come find you. You know I can. You know I will."

Not sure if I say *jeezuz* out loud, but probably. I am sure that I get a wicked trilling from the base of my spine all the way up to the stem of my brain. Internally, it sounds just like an angry xylophone.

"Why are you being creepy?" I ask him.

"Because it's gonna be up to me to teach you to be a

man. So I'm gonna do that. I came to the house to take you out, give you the benefit of my vast experience before high school chews you up and spits you out. It's a shithole, high school, and I'm the only person who can properly prepare you for what's coming."

"Oh, no, thanks anyway," I say. "I'd probably rather be surprised."

"Oh, so you think your little pal there is gonna show you what's what?"

"Hey, there's a thought," I say. "Maybe Cy could be the brother I never had."

He growls, authentically canine style, "If anybody's gonna be the brother you never had, it's gonna be me, asswipe. You got that?"

I'm on the brink of a surely fatal burst of laughter when I have a better idea.

"You still at the house?" I ask.

"Yeah," he says. "Get your ass back here, pronto."

"Okay," I say, "I'll be there."

"I guess you heard all that," I say after hanging up.

"Oh, yeah," he says. "Heading home 'pronto,' are ya?"

"Pronto, *no*," I say.

"Ooh," he says, "look at you, lying to the big scary brother."

"I didn't lie," I say. "I *will* be there. Just not anytime soon. He'll probably be napping, or riding home, by the time he works it out."

"Ah, I like that," he says. "Your brother's an irredeemable asshole and deserves what he gets."

"Yeah," I say, fearing the irredeemable part is true while still hoping it isn't. "I suppose."

"But your sister's sweet."

"Not sure I'd call her that," I say. "I'm not even sure she'd call herself that. But she's all right. You know the saying, you can't choose your family . . ."

He reaches over and slaps me sideways on the shoulder. It knocks me almost flat into the grass, but not as flat as his smile and his words do. "Sure ya can," he says. "I believe that's exactly what you can do."

I'm a little embarrassed and find myself staring at the ground.

"We probably need to get moving," I say as we hop to our feet. The dogs and their escorts walk peacefully across the grass for a couple of minutes. In the opposite direction from home.

I'm feeling pretty proud of myself, messing with Ike rather than my usual crumpling before him. And that Cy was a witness to it. But I'm not feeling so good that I don't snap to attention when I hear the distinctive Harley roar lioning down the big road at the far left of us. I freeze, staring and staring, trying to work out if it's him. I cannot rule it out, but as the machine drifts along and away from us, I remain fixated.

Cy pulls on my sleeve. Then he points downfield. "Hey, ah, I think you lost something."

I look up and then off to where he's pointing. There, Wilbur is flying like a big hairy cloud across the field at a shockingly fast pace. I look to Orville, still grazing the grass next to us but also chewing the remains of the nylon connector that had them yoked together. I jump to it and start frantically pursuing Wilbur, calling out his name. Orville gallops along beside me, with Cy falling in behind us.

"I guess Orville felt bad for holding them both back because of his behavior and decided to set his brother free," Cy says helpfully. Then he starts singing, "Born free . . ."

"Knock it off, Cy," I call. "This is serious. I never lost anybody's dog before."

Hearing that, Cy knocks it right off and takes it seriously. He turns on the jets and blows past me as we lose sight of Wilbur crossing the street. People don't think sheepdogs are fast, but those people are wrong.

Cy reaches the main road and starts scanning right and left to see if the dog went that way. There are several roads across from us where he could have gone, in the direction leading away from the field altogether. I look to Cy with my hands out pleadingly, because I guess I've come to think of him as the answer man somehow. He matches my helpless gesture but crosses the street toward the smaller roads.

Orville and I follow. Before we reach the other side, my phone rings. It's Aggie. I pick it up and am just about to start boo-hooing to her about how I can't talk now because I lost a dog. But she beats me to the boo-hoo.

"What's wrong?" I say, desperately enough that Cy repeats my words.

Her words are not really words. She's very upset, very

un-Aggie. She's asking me to come over, I can just about tell. Her father's gonna kill Lois. Gonna pull all three remaining legs off her like a big bug. Her mother said she could keep the dog, but her father never agreed. Now he's there and her mother's not, and she needs to get out because her father keeps following them around the apartment, being scary, and can I please come over. I'm her friend, can I please come over. I'm her friend.

I'm her friend, is why.

"But?" I honk, gesturing at the dog as if Aggie can see.

Cy has of course heard it all, because he's right there. He grabs Orville's lead. "I'll be needing this," he says. "We'll find Wilbur. Orville will find his brother. You go to your friend."

I'm a couple of strides in the direction of my friend when Cy calls to me, "Oh, y'know, tell her to get out of there. Tell her to go over to my apartment and she can hang with Celia till you get there...."

"Aren't you worried, though? About your ma ... about Aggie's dad ...?"

"Ha-ha," Cy says, leading Orville diagonally across the street. "I almost hope he does try it. Celia will make a meathead pie out of him."

I'm breathless when I come running up the stairs and finally knock on the door. Celia calls for me to come on in, and I feel instantly relieved to see them all there around the table.

The sense of relief has made me a little bold.

"Right," I say. "You want me to go down there and get tough with him?"

I didn't *think* I was joking. Apparently I was the only one who didn't.

They all laugh, even—I am certain—Lois.

"That was good," Agatha says, hopping up and coming to give me a hug. "I needed that."

"Happy to be of service," I say through gritted teeth. Truth is, I'm pleased. I have no idea what would've happened if they'd taken me seriously.

There's waiting to be done. Agatha says she needs to wait for the *change o' shift*. That's when her dad clears out and her mom eventually rolls back in. Then she and Lois can go back home and work out what to do before the old man comes back in a few days. Pierre is here, looking solid and substantial as ever. But he looks bulky and old, too, next to Lois. He's a gracious host, though, seeming unconcerned, or possibly unaware, that company is moving around as he mostly sleeps under the front window.

Cy called and said he and Orville are right on Wilbur's heels—without saying how he knows that—and we're to wait for him to let us know when he's got him.

It's not the most painful way to kill time. Celia really is some kind of master chef and baker. The house smells of all kinds of things I wouldn't be smelling at my house, and the first new sensation she grants us is sweet potato muffins laced with buttery sugar swirls. Agatha and I gobble these in front of the TV while Lois and Pierre make the most of a couple of long rib bones that seemed to be lying in the refrigerator with their names on them. The ribs are long and only slightly curved and if you looked hard it would be easy to see them fitting into the torso of the three-legged dog herself. She's obviously still got her complete set, though. Of ribs, anyway.

We watch silly stuff, mostly cartoons and soap operas, while Celia chirps happily along between us and the kitchen, singing without words and running a mini restaurant without saying much of anything at all. Lois has clued into what's what almost immediately—or just as long as it took her to finish off that bone—and is now hopping along at Celia's elbow every which way she moves. Pierre's mostly a handsome piece of furniture.

There's much to not talk about. And we're doing a mighty job of not talking about it. Finally, when Celia drops lunch down—how did we get to lunch already?—talk becomes unavoidable. "This is amazing," Aggie says. She's waving her spoon around like a magician over the generous helpings of aromatic rice with herbs and green vegetables, red beans and chunks of what I eventually find out is curried goat, long after I've finished eating or cared what it even was. I wave my magician's spoon over it all as well, as if the actual magic hadn't already been done in the kitchen.

"I'm delighted you like it," Celia says. Then, after a gentle pause, "When do you think it'll be safe to go back, Aggie?"

"Oh," Aggie says awkwardly. "I'm so sorry. I'll get going as soon as I'm finished with this gorgeous lunch." She proceeds to start shoveling rice into her mouth.

Celia laughs warmly and slides like a yoga expert into a cross-legged seat on the floor next to Aggie. "No, darlin'," she says, "it's not that I want you to go *now*. Quite the opposite. I want to make sure you don't go back too soon. Not till it's safe. You can stay here as long as you want. The longer the better, as far as I'm concerned."

Aggie gets all pink-face flushed and watery-eyed as she works even faster through her lunch. Celia watches over her, maybe to keep her from choking. I eat as reasonably quickly and silently as I can. Bowls empty, we stare all around at one another for another couple of minutes.

"Stay here indefinitely," Celia says like a solemnly bursting dam. The whole room quakes with the weight of what she's said, though she seems apologetic at the same time.

Celia and Agatha share a kind of maybe female silence I don't understand.

"Yes," I bark, rather generously when you think about it, since I live elsewhere. "It's perfect. You could stay here, Aggie, like, forever." I'm certain Cy would have said the same thing if he were here. Without a doubt, I've picked up something from his Samaritan's-eye view of life.

Aggie is glowering at me. She wants to say something hard to me, but I think she's holding back.

Celia fills in the gap, going to Aggie and holding her, while speaking what should be an obvious truth to me.

"She's not a rescue dog, Louis. It's not that simple."

Now I feel like a bad dog myself. This *getting involved* business is a lot harder than I would have thought. I feel my head drop and my whole body heat up.

"I know you didn't mean it that way," Aggie says when

she sees the state of me. "It's not your fault. You just don't know any better."

That weirdly raises my spirits. "I don't. I really don't."

I so wish for that call from Cy.

Lois angles around behind the ladies sitting on the floor. The dog lies out flat, and it's as flat as a fully formed dog can get. Within seconds, Celia and Agatha lie back, side by side, with Lois as one hairy, bony pillow. Pierre keeps his distance. Within a few seconds more, the three close their eyes.

Taking advantage of this, and the cover of one more dopey soapy TV show, I get up and slip out the door.

Cy doesn't sound all that happy when I reach him on the phone.

"I told you to wait," he says.

"What's going on?" I demand.

There's a long pause.

"It wasn't your fault," he finally says.

"Seems to be a lot of that going around. Where are you?" I ask.

"I'm at the Wright brothers' house."

I find the three of them sprawled on the sprawling porch. Cy's sitting on the top step. Wilbur is laid out, his head on Cy's lap. Orville is lying with his head on his brother's lifeless belly.

It's probably impossible to walk up a flight of eight steps any slower than I do it now.

"Hit-and-run," Cy says before I can ask. "They never

even stopped for him. Poor Wilbur was gone already when I got there."

I stroke Wilbur's lovely hairy face. He looks exactly the same. I go around and stroke Orville. He's motionless, unlike every single other time.

I come back around, take the seat right next to my partner. "They won't be back for at least a couple of hours," I say.

"I'll wait," he says.

"We'll wait," I say.

We sit, we sigh. We sigh some more.

"Two dogs have died on me now," I say.

"They didn't die 'on you,' Louis."

"Yeah, but if I'd just stayed home instead of getting into this dog business, I wouldn't have had to go through this."

"True," he says. "If you just stayed home, you wouldn't have had to go through death. Or life, either, for that matter. Thank dog for that, huh?"

I almost feel like I could laugh at that. Right now, *almost* is good enough.

"This is gonna be *hard*," I say.

"Yes, it is," he says as he puts his arm around my shoulders, completing our extended chain of brothers.

16. Of Human Bondage

IN THE END IT WAS EVEN HARDER.

Who knew it could hurt so much, to hurt someone so much?

Nobody's fault. They are very nice guys, the Wright brothers' parents. I think they wanted to kill somebody, and I suppose I was lucky that they wore themselves out with sobbing. There was the chewed leash as proof and a very sad Orville as a sort of penance. He will have to live from now on with being the most mercilessly loved creature on earth.

When I walk too fast down those porch steps, Cy pulls on the back of my shirt to ensure that I remain more dignified.

Without discussing it, we head back to his apartment, where the four of them are in the kitchen and two of them are working together on some kind of stew for dinner. We tell them. There are more tears.

There is dinner, and suddenly I can't think of a more magnificent word than stew. We all watch more nothing on TV. After dinner, Cy insists on taking Lois and Pierre for a walk around the neighborhood, and I insist on going with them. Nothing bad happens, though I keep expecting it to.

Afterward, we all spread out around the floor. I text Faye and Dad and say I'm with Cy and I'm fine and I'll explain all tomorrow.

Agatha and Lois don't go back to the apartment. Huddling is the thing that feels right. "Good company," Celia quietly announces.

We all sleep right there on the floor together, all night.

I wake up, a little stiff but at the same time feeling like I had the sweetest sleep of my life. Celia's in the kitchen, doing something delicious. Cy and Aggie are already awake, staring at me and giggling about some hilarious remark one of them must have just made. Pierre's draped over Cy. Lois is pacing anxiously between us and the kitchen and back.

For whatever reason—for all the reasons—I'm swamped with thoughts of my mother and how I haven't seen her in what feels like years.

"I gotta go," I say, jumping to my feet.

Celia protests from the kitchen.

"No, thank you for everything, Ms. Toussaint," I say, "but . . . I need to go see my ma right now. You wouldn't want to keep me from that, now, wouldja?"

Unfair but effective. Celia comes out with something heavenly wrapped in napkins. Turns out to be a giant banana-maple fritter, and I can't wait for it to cool down enough for me to devour it.

"Let me come with you," Agatha says, grabbing my arm.

I look at her, about to object, but without a reason. "Lois, too?" I say instead.

"Yes, yes, yes," she says, and starts gathering herself together.

"What about me?" Cy says groggily from the floor. I don't get the impression he slept as well as I did.

"Sure," I say. "You wanna come?"

"Not particularly," he says, grinning. "Just being polite."

He stays politely where he is as Aggie, Lois, and I head out.

"Oh . . . my . . . word," Ma says as we come strolling into her sunny, bright room. The window is wide open, which can only mean good stuff for my traditionally fresh-air-freak mother.

The word she lacks words for is Lois.

"Come here, magnificence," she says, swinging her legs off the bed and extending her arms. Lois hops straight to her and nuzzles straight and deep into her embrace. It's a hug and a half, and my heart races with the sight of it.

"Hello," Ma says to Aggie, like a secret, over Lois's shoulder. "I'm sorry for my rudeness, but what a lovely creature you've got here."

"The creature is Lois, Ma," I say, "and this is my friend Agatha."

"Pleased to meet you, Agatha. Is this your dog?"

"Well, sort of," Aggie says. "It's a long story, but I guess Louis and I sort of have shared custody."

"What?" Ma says, stunned but thrilled.

"What?" I say, more or less the same way.

"Yeah, I was thinking about it," Aggie says. "It might not be safe enough for her at my house. We could, like share her, but mostly she could stay with you. If that's okay?"

I open my mouth to speak, but there's no need.

"Entirely okay," Ma blurts. "Oh, kids, this dog is magical."

"Yeah," Louis says. "Cy says all dogs are magical."

"Well, he's right," she says. "But some are even more magical than others."

And clearly, this is one of those dogs. I haven't seen Ma this lit up since . . . since the before times.

"Are you sure?" I say.

"Of course I'm sure," Ma answers.

"Do you mind, Mother? I was talking to Agatha."

Aggie giggles. "You guys are really funny," she says.

Ma and I both sort of shudder-freeze together.

"People used to tell us that all the time. Remember that, Ma?"

"I remember," she whispers, practically into Lois's ear.

Outside, we start walking together, until we start walking apart.

"Where are you going, Aggie?" I say.

"Home. Where do you think?"

I don't tell her what I think. I simply walk along with her.

"You can't just hover around me all the time," she says. "It is where I live, after all."

Once we get to her building, she hands me Lois's leash.

"So, how are we gonna schedule this joint custody thing?" I ask her.

She shrugs. Pauses, then nearly knocks me to the sidewalk by kissing my cheek.

I must look horrified or scared or something, because she laughs and points at the cheek. "Don't worry, Louis, that was a good thing. Humans do it sometimes. And also, don't worry about me. I'll be fine. Celia says that people just need witnesses, in order to behave themselves. I know I have witnesses, friends and neighbors, looking out for me now. Good company."

17. Guide Dogs

I KNOW THAT IT'S A THING, LIKE IN BOOKS AND MOVIES. That a guy gets kissed by a girl and then he goes all ker-flooey and acts different.

It takes me a full two days to decide that's not what's happening to me. Since that's not what's happening, let's put that aside. But *something* happens that's different. In another first, I have a plan.

I call my brother on the phone.

"Are you kidding me?" is his version of hello, and it almost makes the whole business worthwhile.

"I'm sorry," I say.

"Really? About the fishing thing, you mean?"

"No," I say. "About punking you that I was coming to meet you at the house."

"Oh. Right. And what about the fishing thing?"

It sounds stupid—on both our parts—but I'm sort of surprised and moved to realize he really was hurt by being left out of the fishing trip. Who knew he was capable?

"Sorry about that, too," I say. "How many times do you need me to apologize?"

"I'm thinking . . . seven."

"I believe I'm up to three already. But I'll work on it."

"Okay, good," he says. "That's a start. So what do you want from me? You wouldn't be calling if you didn't want something."

Just when you think you're too clever to be rumbled . . . "Can you come here?" I say.

I have no idea where he was or what he was up to when I phoned him. But there is no lag time between my request and the sound of the Harley bursting to life beneath him. There is also nothing like a *goodbye, I'll be right over,* or—thankfully—*get stuffed, little brother,* before he hangs up.

Shortly, I hear the approach of a loudly rumbling motorcycle.

He does provoke stuff, my brother. That's his history, obviously, of provoking stuff. Reactions, fights, strong opinions from friends, family, and strangers alike. He doesn't even have to try, though he still does, just in case. Right now, he's provoking a wave of fear in me, though I don't have any specific reason for that. I spoke to him only minutes ago, and he was totally okay.

I just don't know, is probably the explanation. Like when you're dealing with another species, and you never can fully know whether they're going to lick your hand or chew it off.

Much as I know my brother, really, I don't.

"If you could just appreciate that all I wanna do is help you, Louis, maybe we'd get along better." See? Like that. Never saw that one coming.

I'm standing in front of our house, and he's sitting on the bike.

"Fine. How are you trying to help me?"

"I'm trying to show you what nobody showed me till it was too late. How vicious high school can be. I'm trying to get to you before they do. Before they do to you what they did to me."

It doesn't sound like much, but it's much. I never heard quite these words. How Ike felt he was so wronged back then. In most tellings—even his own parents'—Ike was the aggressor in high school. If he were a dog, he would have been put down.

"What're you saying, Ike, that you didn't enjoy getting into all those fights?"

He pauses. Which he almost never does. While I'll never ask him, I'd be willing to bet he doesn't even know why a person might take a second before speaking.

"Not at first, I didn't. But I learned. Then I learned more."

I pause. Which is something I frequently do.

"That makes me sad," I say. "Is that what you're trying to teach me? To fight back—but *first*?"

"That's it, exactly," he says excitedly, pointing at me like an explorer spying a new land.

It's odd, as we hang there, almost appreciating each other, coming together while being so far apart.

He means something like well.

"Um, no, Ike," I say. "I'm sorry for how it was for you. But it's gonna be different for me."

He shakes his head slowly, looking like he feels sorry for me. He probably does, but more for my foolishness in not taking his advice than for whatever holy high school hell awaits me. Probably both.

"No, it's not," he says. "Suit yourself . . . your funeral . . ." And further clichés to that effect come out of him, but my mind's moving forward.

"Um, well, this is gonna be some awkward timing," I say, "but I kinda need a goon."

He goes all comically swoony, fanning himself with both hands and fluttering his eyelids. "Really? You mean me?"

I suppose he deserves his moment. "Yes, I do."

"Ha, I've been waiting a long time for this." The words say *joke*, but the eyes say no such thing. "Bet you thought I was gonna be insulted by that," he says.

"You'd lose that bet," I say.

Faye has appeared in front of the house, with Lois on the leash. Aggie and I have worked out a rough schedule of three-day/four-day custody of Lois. Today is trade-off day, and Aggie said she'd come to get her, but I thought we'd get things off on the right foot. We're delivering.

"What do you need me to do?" Ike asks.

"Just come over to Aggie's. Be with us while we hand the dog over. See, we want to make a kind of statement, that she has backup . . . friends and support and—"

"Goons," Ike says brightly.

"I shouldn't have put it like that," I say, without exactly correcting him. "Just this one time, it might be helpful to have your . . . special aura in the vicinity. A show of unity."

"Goonity!" Faye chips in. A real family affair we've got going now.

Faye, Lois, and I walk on over while Ike motors himself there. He's got time to kill, obviously, so he keeps driving one way and back again, like a military flyby before the actual event. I have texted Cy so that he and Celia and Pierre can rendezvous with us. We have timed this so that it is also handover day with Aggie's parents, and we are catching them at the pivot point in their routine that Aggie dreads the most.

Mom is coming and Dad is going, and our company of misfit toys will form a kind of honor guard for the whole thing.

We march up the stairs to Agatha's landing, where the Toussaints link up with us. Ike makes an almost charming little growl at the sight of Cy, like a protective dog protecting something only he can see. But after the initial worry, I'm happy to find Ike prepared to see the bigger picture instead. We march to the door, and Faye rings the bell several times, as arranged.

Also as arranged, Aggie does not come running to the door. It must take all of her considerable strength to hold herself back.

Finally, the Man opens the door. He stands, staring, goggle-eyed, at each of us in turn. He takes it all in, silently. After thirty unlovely seconds, he shuffles past us.

"No, *our* pleasure," says Ike as he passes.

Agatha stands in the doorway. A woman stands a few feet behind her; she's no human bubble bath either, but she nods vaguely our way.

"Your glorious beastie," Faye says, handing the leash to a beaming Aggie. She forgoes the leash and hugs the dog crazy hard around her hairy swan neck.

And that's it. Wordlessly, it.

The door closes on our Great Transaction.

But we don't go anywhere. We linger on the landing, though there's nothing left for us here except to maybe mark the territory a little more emphatically.

Not sure what everybody else is doing, but I'm listening. For what, I'm not sure. Sounds, of happiness, or discontent, or conflict. Sounds that might mean our job isn't done yet. I suppose that's the thing with this getting-involved malarkey—once you're involved, you're involved. Can't walk away, not fully, maybe not ever. I get an actual spine-shudder at the enormity of that thought, and I hope nobody sees it.

There are no untoward sounds.

Until Ike, naturally.

"Well, unlike the rest of ya, I got a life," he says, and makes a military salute before turning on his heel.

We all follow suit, because it is time.

We make our way as a unit, back to the stairway, where the Toussaints go their way and we go ours. They invite us in—I have a moment of shock and horror thinking my brother may accept just to be demonically awkward—but we all politely decline.

As we reach the bike and Ike swings his leg over, he points up in Cy's general direction.

"That was fun," he says, "but I still don't like that kid."

He thunders up the bike and makes sure every corner of the neighborhood feels his presence before hauling away.

Faye and I have a leisurely walk home. It feels like we did more of a something than it probably looks like, and I'm sort of worn out.

"You better be careful," she says.

"Ah, I don't think they'll give us any real trouble," I say. "And anyway, you know what? I'm not even afraid if they do."

She laughs. "I know you're not. That's what I'm talking about. You're in real danger of becoming a real person who does stuff. Meaningful stuff and good stuff."

I feel myself blush a little. "Cut it out," I say. "You're getting carried away."

"No, I'm not. And I blame the dogs. If you never got into the dogs, you'd have never gotten into the whole life-and-death business. They took you there, y'know. All dogs are guide dogs in the end."

She stops talking, right there, because Faye is smarter than me and everybody else. We walk on in quiet, because I almost feel like this might make me cry.

And I am absolutely not ready for any more personal growth of that nature right now.

18. The Orientation Express

DAD WAS A CITY FIREFIGHTER FOR TWENTY YEARS, FROM A year out of high school. Thought he was gonna spend his time saving babies from trees and cats from floods, spend his off time making chili for the other guys. That was his own description of what passed for his ambition. It all changed over time. A couple of good friends got killed in the line of duty while they were messed up on drugs and alcohol. Cat calls went down, false alarms went up, and instead of being applauded as the hero, he spent too many of his callouts dodging rocks and bottles from the street side.

When he took the early-retirement package on the back of his anxiety issues, he bought himself a dinged-up old bucket, when he didn't even know how to tie a decent knot.

It made him a little happy, for a little while.

"Everybody knows you can't run away, you can't hide away," he says in his drifty voice as we drive over to pick up Aggie. "Turns out you can't float away either."

It seems almost as if we're floating, as the rain swamps the windshield like it's a solid mass of water.

"You think that's what you were doing, Dad? You think that's why we came here?"

He keeps his hands on the wheel, and his eyes straight ahead, as he contemplates the water wall. "It's not that whatever troubles you follows you," he says. "It's that the troubles already exist, everywhere. They'll be there when you get there. You simply have to learn to make accommodation with them when you arrive. You can't duck out from life, though, son. You can't."

I know he means both of us. And I know he's ecstatic at even today's move out into the wider world.

It was pouring down when we ran from the house to the car, and it's pouring down as we pull up in front of Agatha's building.

"I never should have bought that boat," Dad says to his damp shoes.

"Ma told you that, Dad," I say.

"She did," he says, like a human mud puddle. "Everything smart I ever didn't do was told to me by your mother."

"I miss her so much," I say.

"So much," Dad says.

I don't relish getting any wetter, so I sit there looking out at Aggie's apartment building.

"So," Dad says with an obvious lack of anxiety, "I'm selling the boat."

I feel like I should protest this, at least for show. But we all know he's doing the right thing.

"I shoulda just retired after the fire service. Stayed at

home, spent more time with your mother. She'll be happy with this. Aw, hell, she's already happy with it. I couldn't wait to tell her."

"Great, Dad. Awesome. You can be there now when she gets home," I say hopefully. "To look after her."

We smile big and knowingly at each other before he makes the correction.

"I will be there, and be just pathetic enough, so that she can enjoy taking care of *me*," he says. "Your mother does not care to be a *caree*."

I don't love the idea of going out and getting drenched again. We sit for another minute.

Cy springs up and bangs on the window. I jump, the way he wanted me to.

"Thanks," I shout to him. Then Pierre launches himself at the window. I jump again. Dad laughs, at all of it.

"I'm gonna go get Aggie," I say, throwing open the door.

As I do, Cy piles into my seat, followed by Pierre. The door slams, the windows fog immediately up, and I go for my friend. Leaving my other friend—I have two!—with my father.

It takes twenty knocks at the door to get Agatha to appear. I hear lots of snappish conversation in there before she comes out and slams the door behind her. She grabs my hand tight, and it feels like she's trying to pull me *through* the stairs as we make our way back down to Dad's car.

"Thought you said both your parents were working?" I say. "That's why they couldn't come today."

"Shush," she says, with the finger at the lips and everything.

As long as we're going retro, I do the lock-and-key gesture at my own lips.

"I don't think I've ever been this excited about anything in my whole life," she says. I can't work out whether she's talking about the thing we're headed toward or the thing we're escaping. They both make me so sad I could squeal.

When we get to the car, the window fog is so thick it might as well be cake frosting. I yank the door open, and they have clearly been discussing big, weighty matters.

"Ah, well," Cy says, "I learned a lesson. Damned if I know what the lesson was, but I learned a thing anyway."

"Life's a long song," Dad says. "Keep listening and learn it all."

"Wow, what'd I miss?" Aggie says as I pull Cy out of the front seat and Pierre follows. I install her in their place and shut the door crisply.

"Where you guys going?" Cy asks me.

"Orientation at the school," I say.

"Cool. Want me to come along?"

"Ah, thanks anyway, but you're already orientated. It's just for rookies. If I showed up with you, it would kinda be like going to a cycling lesson with my training wheels still on."

"Good point," he says as I pile into the back of the car. "And I suppose one chaperone is plenty for any date."

"Shut up, it's not a date," I say, slamming my door.

Dad and Agatha are both giggling as we pull away from the curb.

· · ·

The high school appears to be nothing special. Redbrick and low slung, set on a small grassy hill, it could be a potato chip factory or a minimum-security prison. My last school was a lot smaller but had far more charm. My mother lived there.

But this is special. It's obvious from the start.

Maybe it's that sweet sensation you get when torrential rains fade into drizzle, then mist, then tentative sunshine. The place transforms right in front of us as we pull into the parking lot, and Agatha bounces in her seat as if we're arriving at a huge party being thrown in her honor.

Not only does she not wait for Dad to park before unbuckling and rolling out of the car like we're a SWAT team or something, but I'm pretty sure the car hasn't come to a full stop by the time she throws my door open and yanks me along with her.

"Dad? Help?" I plead.

"No way," he says, appearing positively thrilled with what is happening to me.

"He'll catch up," Aggie says, hauling me by the hand across the lot. It's about one-third filled with cars, with a number of less deranged people getting out of them and filing toward the building in an orderly fashion.

We fairly crash through the big front doors and find ourselves in an open and bright foyer ringed in glass cases full of trophies and photos and plaques. Aggie pulls me around the cases, investigating the vast achievements of students past and present, calling out random words that excite her. "Debate," she squeals, "that's for sure. Volleyball, yessir. Badminton, soccer . . . we're gonna be sooo busy, Louis. Football, absolutely not. Barbaric. Wrestling, though. You could do that. . . ."

"No, I couldn't," I cough. She's close to scaring me here, but she's even closer to making me burst out laughing. She yanks me ever harder around the trophy cases, and I start yanking back. She hardly seems to notice.

Dad appears beside me. "Very impressive," he marvels, looking all around. "I had no idea."

"Neither did I," I say. "Apparently, I'm gonna be a wrestler."

He does a double take. "Yeah," he says. "Sure, I can see that."

I see his double take and raise him a take. "Uh-huh," I say, "neither can I."

He laughs. "Right, neither can I."

Agatha is practically running past the remaining cases and up the six steps toward the gym. She's tugging me like a balloon behind her, and Dad's following close, like I'm a balloon with its own balloon.

"What's the rush?" Dad calls, laughing as Aggie shoves the gym door aside. The place is buzzing, tables set up like booths all around the perimeter of the place. It feels like an arts fair or a Christmas market, though all the stations are manned by teachers and administrators and coaches touting different classes and clubs and extracurricular whatsits for our freshman consideration. Families rolling around clockwise and counter are pleasantly bumping into one another under the watchful eyes of basketball hoops retracted to the ceiling and championship banners only slightly muffling the hubbub hubbubing at us off the glazed yellow tiles of all four walls.

"Easy, Aggie," I say, gently but loud enough to be heard, as I pull on her powerful arm.

She stops, finally, and whirls around to face me.

Tears are rolling down her cheeks, and I'm instantly lumping in my throat at the sight of her.

"What's wrong?" I choke out.

"I'm so happy," she says.

Oh. No. Oh no.

I don't understand it. At all. I don't understand her, and I don't understand me. Happiness shouldn't make a person cry. And her happiness shouldn't make . . . whatever's happening to me happen.

I knew I shouldn't have come here. This is a disaster.

I reach out and touch her shoulders. I must have seen that move in a movie or something. "You'll be fine," I say.

"This place is so remarkable," she says. "I'll get to start all over again here."

I see it now, in her face. She is hugely, deeply, madly happy. She has reached out to me and grabbed two mighty handfuls of my shirt, at my waist, as she says this.

It feels as if she's giving me credit somehow for all of it.

The three of us make a whistle-stop tour of all the tables, hearing pep talks about the advantages of taking Spanish over French and vice versa, chemistry over biology, geography over history. Then a guidance counselor points out that that's all conversation for another day, another year, because our class choices have already been made for us for this year.

"But don't they make you feel *wanted*?" Aggie says. "Like you're being recruited to play on a team because you're really good at something?"

I shrug agreeably, sending her into a happy dance of shruggery and a brand-new fit of giggles at my expense.

We come around to the tables where we might have real choices to make, activity clubs and intramural sports and such, and here Dad leans in close and even starts asking questions, which means I'll get an earful later. Double doors at the back of the hall spring open, and crowds of frosh flow like ants out through them.

"What's going on there?" I ask.

"Who cares?" she says, yanking me along.

For once, I nearly match her enthusiasm, slapping my dad on the back and leaving him achieving the near impossible by visibly boring the chess club coach with questions.

We step outside into the vastness of the school's sports facilities. It's hard not to be impressed. There's a full football field, surrounded by an eight-lane red running track, which is surrounded by a semicircle of stands. There are ten sky-high towers distributed around the oval, topped with banks of lights for night games.

"Can you believe it?" Aggie says. "I mean, I always saw this stuff from a distance, from our side of the hills, but up close . . . it's amazing, how *big* the world can be, Louis."

"Don't remind me," I say.

I'm managing to hold to my grouchiness in the face of

Aggie's complete joy and wonder. But I must confess, it's taking more effort than I would have imagined.

Orientees are flocking and flapping around in a way that reminds me of my previous academic orientation . . . in preschool. Just as we're reaching the point of feeling a little bit big around town, this here is putting us right back to little in short order.

There are some authority types down on the track, calling stuff out to the new kids. These are various coaches and gym teachers and club leaders; it's easy to tell because they dress and move much more like us than like the grown-ups of the staff. And also, the whistles.

Several whistles are screeched, and the crowd gathers closer.

"No pressure, kids, just have fun. But this does give us a chance, in a highly unscientific way, to get an idea of who's who in our incoming class. Just a quick peek, you understand, at your basic level of fitness and competency . . ."

"That's it," I say, turning up toward the auditorium again. "I'm outta here."

Before I can even grasp what's happening, Aggie has grasped me. I'm in the middle of the throng, but I'm the only one walking backward, which makes me even more awkward and obvious than I would be on my own. "All right," I say to her, twisting loose.

"It'll be fun," she says. "You'll see."

"It won't, and I won't."

"You'll do it for me, then," she says.

"Why would I do that?" I say.

But that is exactly what I proceed to do, and why I do it.

Whistles blow, students are randomly selected, and a big group of us lines up in lanes. Seconds pass like years, finally a gunshot goes off, and because I don't drop dead on the spot, I run, along with everybody else.

The other kids who will or will not run later erupt in mad cheering, as if they care a hoot about who finishes where in this heat. Because it's been a while since I've run anywhere on purpose, I'm finding this exercise to be alarmingly odd and difficult. The things that came so naturally as a young, young kid are not doing that now. I'm thinking seriously about things like coordinating arms and legs, about breathing in and breathing out and whether my stomach should actually be bulging forth at any point in the process.

We were told at the start that the track is four hundred yards around, and I swear it must take me eight steps to cover each one of them. Even in my heyday—which I never had—I don't think I ran this distance in one go. By the halfway mark I'm getting hamstring cramps, and a hundred yards farther, stomach cramps. This whole thing is some kind of assessment process, like Harry Potter's Sadistic Sorting Hat of Sports, and as we head down the final straightaway, we can see the various coachy types pointing and commenting and making notes on the clipboards those guys are required by law to carry at all times.

Of the twenty-four starters in the race, eighteen or so are already in the metaphorical showers by the time I cross the survival-embarrassment line. Aggie has had enough time to cross, double back, and do a few toe-touchies before applauding and woo-hooing me and my ilk to finish.

She gives me a sweet hug, which I am too weak and winded to resist. Then she continues past me to go up to each of the truly committed stragglers, shaking their hands and telling every one what a great job they did.

They did not. Okay, *we* did not. And I know I do myself no favors when I say that each one of these tail-end athletics looks exactly like you would imagine them to. My father awaits their return to the chess club table.

But that's not where they go. Not right away, anyway. For now, something remarkable happens. As a group, they fall in line behind Agatha. They follow every left-right twitch she makes as she congratulates the real winners and politely fields inquiries from various team coaches on her future sporting plans.

I realize that, like the also-sorta-rans, I'm trailing in Agatha's slipstream. I halt suddenly and just observe.

She has entranced these kids. With attention. With that infuriating *spirit* of hers.

With kindness.

"Where you going now?" asks one boy who is roughly nine feet tall and speaks from behind a mystery curtain of silky white hair.

"I don't know," she says brightly. "I think they're doing tours of the classrooms and art studio and labs and library. Wanna do that?"

Five different kids erupt in the affirmative, as if each one has received the one and only valentine she's given out this year.

As she leads the procession back up to the building, I rush up and grab her elbow. "What are you doing?" I say, making a sly head gesture at the gang.

"Isn't it great?" she bubbles. "They can be our pack. We've got a pack already, Louis."

She's misting up again. But I must hold firm. "No. No pack," I insist. "Pretty sure we discussed this pack thing already."

"Pretty sure we didn't," she says as we reach the door, which has just banged shut in front of us. She stares at it, clearly sensing her current level of power. "Are you going to be a gentleman and get that door for me?" she says.

"I didn't need you to tell me," I say. "I was already gonna do it."

I yank the door and stand holding it, like an oaf.

"You're jealous," she says, passing me by, "and that's very sweet."

I find myself involuntarily growling as a geek creek flows past me. I scowl at everybody with an unmistakable *you'll miss me when I'm gone* flourish.

"Not jealous," I say out loud.

But . . . possessive, maybe? Is that what this feeling is?

When did *that* happen?

How did that happen?

I scurry to catch up.

19. Lost and Found

NOT FOR THE FIRST TIME, I WISH I WERE MORE CANINE.

Pierre is more dog than just about anybody. If he were a human movie star, he'd be that sensitive ruffian everybody falls for even while they're a little afraid of him. Ma gets that about him, even though in my mind she's not afraid of anything on earth.

It's Friday of Labor Day weekend. Only another week to go. Beyond that is school. Real school. Cy and I have been talking about it since orientation day. A lot. I'm ready. I'm not. I am.

I have him, and I have Agatha. Ready, I am.

Cy and I step off the elevator and head down the hall for Pierre's weekly swoon-a-thon with my mother. We're not halfway there when we're hit with a gentle wave of music. Harmonica music.

"What's she doing here?" I ask the hallway.

"I don't even know who 'she' is, never mind why she's here," says Cy.

"Agatha," I say. "That's her playing the music."

"Well then," he says, "I'm glad she's here. Sounds sweet. What are you getting irritated about?"

"Just . . . because . . . I like things the way they're supposed to be. Surprises don't thrill me."

Cy starts shaking his head and laughing. He looks down and pretends to be talking to his dog, but he's not fooling me. "If he keeps talking, Pierre, they might not let him leave the hospital when it's time to go."

"It's not a hospital," I say.

"Sorry," he says. "I guess I was confused by all the, y'know, hospitaliness."

"Behave, please," I say as we enter Ma's room.

The music stops as Cy and I go to Ma's bedside.

"Hello, lads," she says, raspy but enthusiastic. She beckons Pierre to her, but he was already in the process of beckoning himself. She makes a high "oof" sound as he lands on her, but she giggles anyway.

It's then I notice, her bag is on the floor next to her. And she's got her traveling duds on.

"You might want to change your mind on surprises," Cy says.

"Ma?" I say.

She's laughing as she roughs up Pierre's roughy head. "Dogs really are magical," she says.

"They really are," Cy concurs. "Magical."

"They really are," Aggie agrees. "Magical."

"Ma?" I say.

She stands, hugs me, and whispers, "Well, I had to be

home to walk my wee boy to his first day of school," she says.

"Maaaa," I gasp.

"You guys really are too funny," Aggie says. "But you might want to know, he has a pod now, so . . ."

"Aggie," I snap.

"I can tell that already," Ma says. Then she quotes a quote. It's from the entrance to the shelter, A Woman's Place.

"'The journey must be made in the company of others,'" she says, beaming sneakily at me. Drives me nuts, the sneaky beam.

She's quoted it countless times. But it was different before.

Ma maneuvers me to the window, where all of us look down on our car, with Dad and Faye and Lois all there, not-so-sneakily beaming up at us. I let my mother take me, like that wee boy, close to her in a big squeeze.

"Magical," we say together.